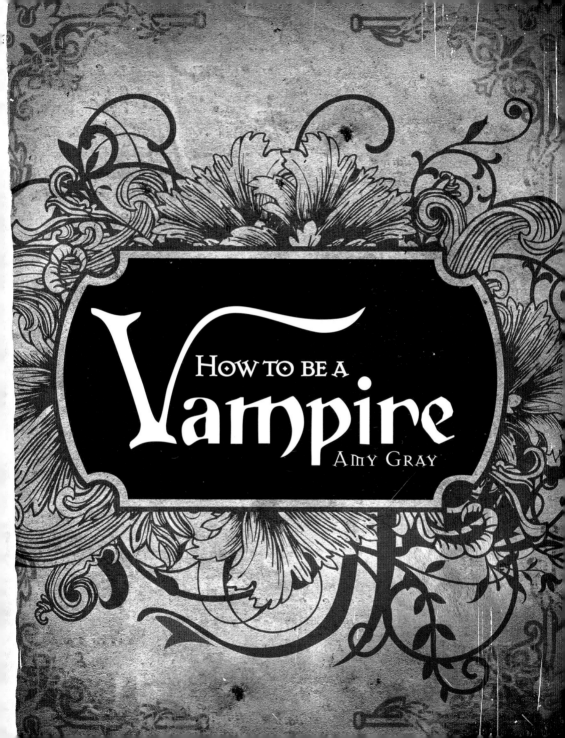

# How to be a Vampire

### Amy Gray

CANDLEWICK PRESS

# A WORLD OF POWER AND BEAUTY AWAITS

## FEARSOME AND IRRESISTIBLE, THE VAMPIRE'S REALM ENTICES

**D**are to escape the scratched confines of mortality? To delude the aging glare of the sun and embrace the night? To assume the mantle of a deity with powers rich beyond your compare? Turn away from the shallow superficiality of today's transient boredom: the perma-tans, the gloss and veneer. Snarl at the everyday, the every person: Become a vampire.

Vampires, lonely gods of night, ascend to a life beyond the mundane triviality of their fragile human brethren. Free from the binds of convention, they taste the taboo and explore the dark. Vampires are humanity perfected. They exude all a human desires: beauty, wiles, youth, gifted strength, and a hip-wiggling, sirenesque seduction in all they do.

Embrace the darkness as the vampires do. Despite their silent pulse, inside every vampire lies a true passion for life—a nightly celebration of their heightened senses and flawless beauty.

People think they know all there is to vampires. They have not bathed under the moon like you will. You will know the truth.

Meander across to the darkened path. Claim beautiful immortality as your prize.

# Contents

## Book One: Leaving the Mortal Realm

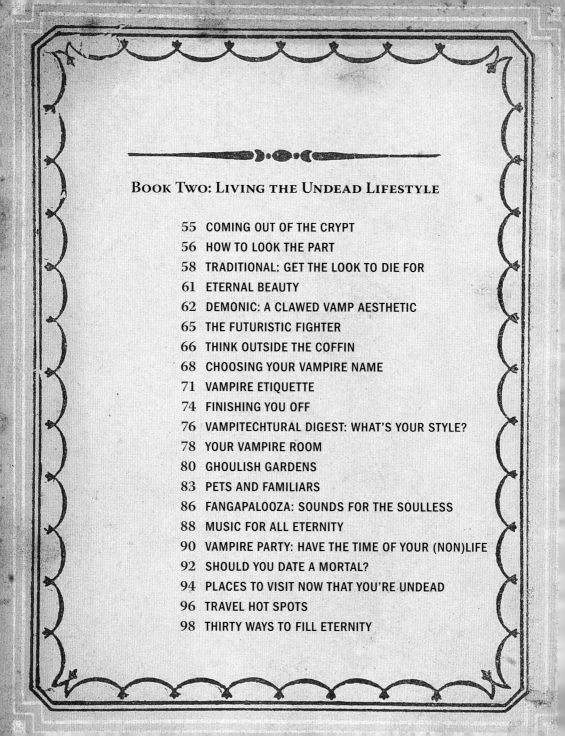

## Book Two: Living the Undead Lifestyle

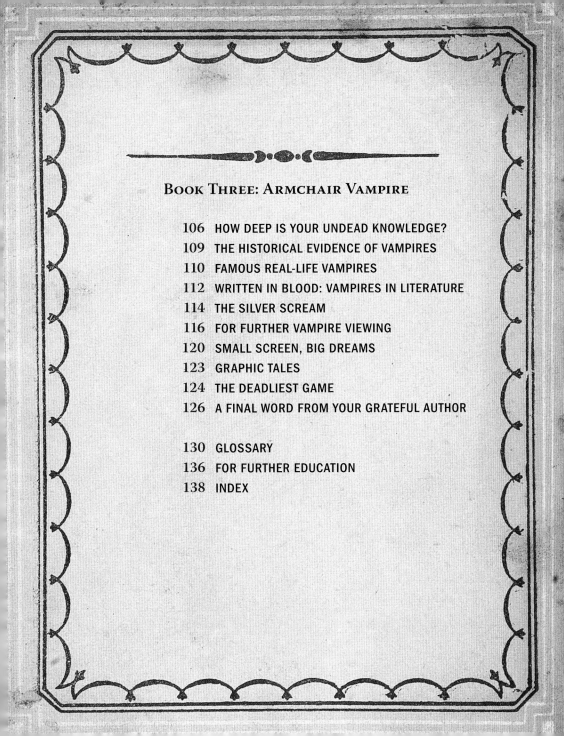

## Book Three: Armchair Vampire

# Leaving the
# Mortal Realm

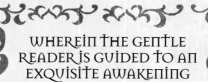

### Wherein the Gentle Reader is Guided to an Exquisite Awakening

**Y**ou stand on the brink of transformation, ready to receive the Dark Embrace and take your place among the Children of Night.

Now that you have made your choice to enter the shadows, a new world awaits. A world imbued with supernatural powers and filled with allies, foes, and, most important, food.

The pages that follow share the secrets of this world: Finding a suitable sire and forging a family to stand with you through the ages. How to unearth your new powers as a fledgling and ways to slake your thirst. And, given that even the undead face hazards and snares, you will learn to protect your precious gift of immortality.

Read on to discover the trials and passions that you will encounter only in the darker realm.

# WHAT'S YOUR VAMPIRE
# PERSONA?

What will you be like once you've made the leap from mere mortal to vampire? Does your vision of eternity involve gothic mansions or abandoned warehouses? Would you rather date, protect, or feed on humans? It's time to find out who you are—or who you will become. Take this quiz to uncover your true vampire type!

## How Do You Like Your Steak?
A. You're a vegetarian.
B. Only the finest, rarest cuts.
C. Raw.
D. Whatever. Food is unimportant.

## When a Vampire Approaches, You
A. Welcome her into your home.
B. Expect him to kneel in deference.
C. Wonder which faction she's from.
D. Brace yourself for a fight.

## Those Closest to You Are
A. Your family members.
B. Your bodyguards.
C. Fellow soldiers.
D. Nobody really knows you.

## Your Idea of the Perfect Night Is
A. Quietly watching over the one you love, even when they're sleeping.
B. Being worshipped by your subjects.
C. Polishing your guns.
D. Riding your motorcycle—fast.

## When You See a Werewolf, You
A. Arrange a truce—but make sure your family has got your back.
B. Do nothing. Shapeshifters are of little concern to you.
C. Grab your arsenal of weapons.
D. Fade into the darkness.

## Your Favorite Outfit Is
A. Whatever high school students are wearing this century.
B. The finest gowns from Paris.
C. Form-fitting black vinyl and leather.
D. Motorcycle jacket, jeans, and big black boots.

## Go on, Share Your Superpowers. What Are You Good at?
A. Resisting temptation—and impersonating a teenager.
B. As a master of diplomacy, you can smooth over any situation.
C. You're a superb, unsurpassed fighting machine.
D. You're an ultimate survivor. You live in the shadows and steal everything you need.

## Mostly A's:
## You're the Family Type

Nothing is more important to you than family and, once someone gets under your skin, you will go to the ends of the earth to protect them. You may appear arrogant to outsiders, but only because you need to protect your sensitive heart.

## Mostly B's:
## You're the Regal Type

You are a refined vampire, gifted with diplomacy and adept at forging intimate bonds with those around you. As a king or queen, your physical attractiveness and intelligence are outstanding. Both mortals and immortals are among your conquests.

## Mostly C's:
## You're the Warrior Type

Tough, bitter, and determined: that's you all over. You're a fighting machine who lives for battle. Proficient with weapons, you have joined the elite ranks of the vampire army. You enjoy spending time in loud nightclubs and deserted warehouses.

## Mostly D's:
## You're a Rebel

You don't follow anyone's rules, mortal or immortal. You may hang with a gang of equally tough and iconoclastic vamps, or set out on your own, roaming the world. Mortals are drawn to your wild-child charm, but you see them only as a source of tasty blood.

# KNOW YOUR
# VAMPIRES

The world is filled with a stunning multitude of bloodsuckers. First recorded in Babylonian times, vampires have roamed every continent on the planet for centuries. What follows is a sampling of vampiric variations, although myriad new types continually evolve and arise, some of which still evade the consciousness of even the most dedicated vampire scholars. Others, however, have left behind unmistakable calling cards. Consider this your shadowed field guide.

TRADITIONAL

### Traditional Vampire

An undead human changed into a demon. Known for devastating charm and style, traditional vampires are powerful hunters with a serious need for blood.

**Habitat** Some require cursed earth from their homeland. Others live in crumbling castles or nice crypts.

**Physical characteristics** Pale skin, cool body temperature, exaggerated canines or incisors, and a razor-sharp manicure.

**Powers** Flight, shapeshifting.

**Weaknesses** Not fond of sunlight, crosses, garlic, or wooden stakes.

RAKSHASA

## ♯ Rakshasa

A blood-seeking ghoul who enjoys the finer things in life, like feeding off pregnant women and helpless babies.

**Habitat** Prevalent around Hindu cemeteries and temples where they heckle priests and attending worshippers.

**Physical characteristics** Fanged, come in a range of colors, and have poisonous nails and a powerful odor.

**Powers** Can shapeshift, show amazing nocturnal strength, and be really, really annoying.

**Weakness** Their strength diminishes at dawn.

MODERN

## ⚱ Modern Vampire

Sleek, sexy, and oh-so-stylish, the modern vamp has it all—except a heartbeat.

**Habitat** Can be found in goth clubs and abandoned warehouses.

**Physical characteristics** Commonly dressed in black, the modern vampire often appears as the undead version of a human metrosexual or hip fashionista.

**Powers** Superstrength, agility, coordination, ability to regenerate, and heightened senses.

**Weakness** Doesn't get along well with werewolves. At all.

## ♄ Chiang-shih

Created from a violent death and a lack of homeland burial, this hopping corpse has a vicious appetite for humans.

**Habitat** Sighted throughout China.

**Physical characteristics** The *chiang-shih* hops and has pale skin and a long tongue. Some may give off a greenish glow and wear long white beards.

**Powers** Enhanced hearing. Stronger *chiang-shih* may fly and shapeshift.

**Weaknesses** They're blind and dislike running water as well as feng shui, garlic, salt, rice, and bells.

CHIANG-SHIH

BAOBHAN SITH

## ♀ Baobhan Sith

She's a bad woman who loves a good hunter. After exhausting a man through dance, she opens up his neck and sucks his veins dry.

**Habitat** The Scottish Highlands.

**Physical characteristics** Astoundingly beautiful due to her elfin heritage.

**Powers** Nails that transform into talons, the ability to shapeshift into a wolf, glamours (a gift that allows this she-demon to hypnotize her victims), and telepathy.

**Weakness** Iron can harm her, so men in the saddle are protected by their iron horseshoes (if they can resist her beauty).

## ⚔ Draug

These Viking undead climb from their graves to drink human blood and drive nearby animals mad with fear.

**Habitat** Found in Viking burial mounds or wreaking havoc in nearby villages.

**Physical characteristics** Death-black or corpse-pale skin.

**Powers** Immune to traditional weapons, they possess indefatigable strength.

**Weaknesses** They consider it a bad day if their heads are cut off and their bodies burnt to ashes and scattered across the sea.

DRAUG

CHUPACABRA

## ⚜ Chupacabra

Cryptozoologists dream of learning more about this nasty beastie—the elusive goatsucker of the Americas.

**Habitat** Mostly Latin America, with some sightings as far north as Maine.

**Physical characteristics** Gray-green, with fangs, spikes, and red eyes. Hops like a kangaroo and is smelly.

**Powers** Its glowering eyes can induce nausea in humans.

**Weaknesses** Scared away by cameras, video recorders, or any other type of recording equipment.

**ROYAL VAMPIRE**

## ⅄ Royal Vampire

Undead royalty who through the centuries have held court over the vampire population, enforcing rules and punishing dissenters.

**Habitat** Hidden chambers under Europe's ancient capitals.

**Physical characteristics** Unearthly beauty and good Italian suits.

**Powers** Uniquely gifted with individual psychic powers such as enhanced mind reading and the ability to mentally transmit confusion, pain, and sensory deprivation to their victims.

**Weaknesses** Rare humans may have mysterious resistance to their powers.

## ⅄ Lamatsu

One of the first vampires, the demon goddess Lamatsu drained the blood of scores of babies, pregnant women, and young men.

**Habitat** Ancient Mesopotamia.

**Physical characteristics** Pale and cold as marble. Sometimes rumored to have furry wings.

**Powers** The daughter of the sky god Anu, Lamatsu inherited the power of flight.

**Weaknesses** Charms that invoke the powers of Pazuzu, a fellow god and the only one to defeat her in battle.

**LAMATSU**

## ᒪ Kêr

Once known as the "Dogs of Hades" given their success at filling the underworld with the dead, these goddesses of violent death took their fill of human blood.

**Habitat** The battlefields of ancient Greece.

**Physical characteristics** These clawed, winged sprites have gnashing teeth and blood-stained robes.

**Powers** Despite their status as minor demons in the ancient Greek pantheon, they cannot be overpowered, only outrun.

**Weaknesses** May be kept away by purification rites.

## Tlahuelpuchi

All families have secrets. This is especially true for families cursed with a *tlahuelpuchi* relative. If a family member kills or identifies their kin as a vampire, the curse will transfer to them.

**Habitat** Native to Mexico.

**Physical characteristics** Most often female, the *tlahuelpuchi* may hunt in the form of a vulture.

**Powers** Able to fly, shapeshift, and hunt without their legs.

**Weaknesses** Sensitive to metal, garlic, and onions.

## Rabisu

These ancient vampiric demons are part of Hell's welcoming committee, pouncing on newly arrived souls.

**Habitat** Hell, especially the entrance. The odd few escape to the land of the living, where they lurk in doorways and dark corners.

**Physical characteristics** Few accounts exist of these devilish creatures, although they are mentioned in both the Christian Bible and Mesopotamian tales.

**Powers** Surprise attack.

**Weaknesses** The only defense against these elusive vampires is pure sea salt.

YARA-MA-YHA-WHO

## ⚡ Yara-ma-yha-who

It's an age-old love story. Girl meets monster; monster sucks girl's blood, eats her, and vomits her up repeatedly until she becomes a monster. Doesn't it make you tear up?

**Habitat** Native to Australia.

**Physical characteristics** With their tiny stature, red skin, toothless grin, and bloodsucking tentacles, they're almost cute.

**Powers** Trickery and magical vomiting.

**Weaknesses** Neither the fastest runner nor all that smart. A bit slow on all counts, apparently.

## ⚡ Manananggal

The beautiful *manananggal* prefers to feast on the blood of pregnant women.

**Habitat** The Philippines.

**Physical characteristics** Often appears as a beautiful woman, although sometimes in two parts.

**Powers** Able to sever her body in two, sprouting wings and leaving her legs behind.

**Weaknesses** Applying salt or garlic to the separated body will kill the vampire and keep it from re-forming.

MANANANGGAL

# How to Be Turned
## All the mad, bad, and crazy ways to become a vampire

You want to be turned. Just as there are myriad vampire types, so, too, are there many ways to be turned. Although folklore emphasizes painful and frightening methods, today's aspiring vampire benefits from greater knowledge and a wealth of options.

### The Vampire's Kiss

Traditionally the dark gift is bestowed when a human and vampire share the most visceral of drinks: each other's blood. This method is fraught with issues and is also incredibly dangerous. What if your sire can't stop drinking?

### Lucky Number 7?

If you're the seventh son of a seventh son (or the seventh daughter of a seventh daughter), the odds are that you are a vampire. The power of numbers imprints a mighty psychic disturbance on the seventh child—for good or for evil.

### Growing Pains

If you have a vampire relative somewhere in your family tree, merely going through adolescence can turn you into a vampire. The powerful hormones that are released during this time speed the body's development into something completely new. Are you sleeping all day? Avoiding others? Not hungry at dinnertime? Could you be a vampire and just not realize it?

### Find Someone Energetic

Psychic vampires, or vampires who feast on the energy of others, are often born from being drained of vitality. The act of draining and refueling (feasting on the emotions of another person) creates a hunger cycle that is only sated by consuming more psi-energy.

### Get Infected

Some vampirologists believe that vampirism is a viral illness that can be passed on from vamps to the general populace. Venom, secreted from the vampire's fangs, moves quickly to incapacitate and take hold of the infected person's body. This is a painful transformation and not for the faint of heart.

### Look to Your Mother

Did your mother not eat enough salt during pregnancy? If so, you can thank her for making you a vampire. This Romanian belief is possibly tied to salt deficiency, which leads to a seriously unquenchable thirst. Other signs, such as being born with a tail, teeth, or a caul may also indicate that you are destined to be a vampire.

### Take a Bath

According to Malaysian legend, if a man disturbs a woman while she meditates in a large wooden bath, she will leap into the air so high that her head will separate from her body. The shock is so great she turns into the *penanggalan*, the demonic flying vampire head of Malaysia.

# Finding the Perfect Sire

I t's an undeniable bond. Your sire acts as a parent, birthing you into a new life. Given the eternal ties between a sire and a vampire, it's a choice you must make wisely. You can find potential sires—both male and female—in a variety of places. Just be sure that the relationship is safe and is founded on mutual interest and respect. Vampire literature abounds with tales of cruel, selfish, and bloodthirsty sires who are doing no favors when they "turn" a mortal.

## Where to Meet Sires

### Stay in School

Your perfect sire may be closer than you think. Vampires that underwent transformation when they were teenagers still look young, and some even attend school so they can blend in with the local community. Take a look around—are there any potential vamps at your school?

### Enjoy the Nightlife

Vampires are often known for their cultural and artistic interests. Movies, concerts, plays, and performances usually take place after dark. If you enjoy a robust cultural life (particularly one that takes you to all-age dance or music clubs) chances are you'll eventually run into one of the undead.

### Do Your Research

Vampires may have superhuman abilities, but there is one thing they're not immune to: flattery. If you spend some time researching vampires, you may find that your interest attracts someone with uncanny knowledge of vampiric life. One thing to

remember: Although technology can help you find like-minded souls, use the same common sense you would about any online interaction. Be sure to protect your personal information and be cyber-safe. If someone you meet online wants personal details or webcam time or pressures you to meet, they're not a sire, just a pervert.

# ARE YOU FOOD OR A COMPANION?

## BECOME FRIENDS

Some vampires are looking for a meal, not a companion, and will weave beguiling lies to get you on the menu. To be sure you're not just a snack, take steps to really get to know each other. You will potentially spend eternity with your sire, and your mortal characteristics will grow more pronounced once you become a vampire. So show him the real you: your gifts, what makes you unique, and why his life will be better with your eternal presence. If you feel like he respects you and is interested in your life (and vice versa), then maybe you've found a perfect match.

## BE SAFE

Until you're certain your sire longs for you as a companion and not as an hors d'oeuvre, insist on meeting in public, well-populated, and well-lit places for your initial courtship. Give it several months and take it slow. This time will help you safely get to know one another and assess the suitability of your relationship. If she agrees and sticks to this, you will know she has higher intentions. Make sure it's *your* decision to be turned.

## GET A TASTE OF THE UNDEAD LIFE

Find ways to get to know your sire candidate's lifestyle, as it's likely to be the sort of life you'd share together. Sometimes vampires will employ mortals as apprentices before turning them. By running errands during the daylight hours, you can become a trusted ally who proves your worth and understands the vampire world before undergoing the transformation. It's equally important to let your sire share of himself. Why does he want a companion, what is his history, and how does he like to live, travel, and feed? If you feel a connection, then you may have just met the most transforming person, which is the best sort of friend anyone (mortal or immortal) could have. Just remember, it's all right to take it slow; you've got eternity on the other side.

# AM I DATING A VAMPIRE?

he ache of searching is over. You've finally found that perfect someone. But is it too good to be true? Could it be that you're having the time of your life with a timeless one? Keep your eye out for these ten signs, and choose your fate. . . .

## HE DOESN'T HAVE A TAN

How can a boy be so pale? His flawless skin is near translucent from his UV-shunning ways. Your sweetheart hides from the sun. In fact, he avoids anything to do with daylight hours or sunny weather. What's he afraid of? Premature aging or premature bursting into flames?

## YOU ONLY GO ON DATES AT NIGHT

She may be the girl of your dreams at night, but during the day? She's constantly sleeping in and never turning up at lunch dates. In fact, she seems to sleep the day away, only coming to life (and your side) at night. Just a sleepy girl? Or fatigued after a night of hunting?

## DINNER DATES? NOT SO MUCH

Have you seen this boy eat? Or does he order something, only to play with his food all evening? How is it he's always claiming a "special diet," feigns lack of appetite, or declares with a smirk that he's "just eaten"? If he's not tempted by the most succulent of dishes and can never slake his thirst, the odds are he has an eating disorder of the most dangerous kind.

## SHE'S AN OLD-FASHIONED GIRL

Does your girlfriend sometimes use outdated expressions or funny words? Is she familiar with corsets, carriages, and calling cards? If her exquisite manners are matched only by her sense of protocol, your sweetie may be supernatural. Depending on when she was turned, these manners may have been retained from an earlier era. Even if she's tried to stay current with the times, her sense of formality will give her away, as vampires have evolved a rigid code of behavior over thousands of years.

## BITTEN BY THE LOVE BUG? OR BY YOUR BOYFRIEND?

Who knew that dating your fellow would drive you to reinvent the turtleneck trend single-handedly? Every time you and that boy start to kiss, he can't stop making a meal out of your neck. With each kiss and moment of passion fraught with desire and loss of blood, is it any wonder that your boyfriend refers to a make-out session as "lunchtime"? Maybe he's just an especially passionate chap, or maybe he finds you really, really delicious.

### He Reminisces About the Old Days—the *Really* Old Days

It's one thing to be a history buff, but this boyfriend has a way of making history come alive. He talks about the end of the Crimean War as if he'd been there and refers to historical figures as if they were old friends. Does he simply have a love of history? Suffer from a mental illness? Harbor delusions of time travel? Or was he there? Look for clues: A collection of antiques and art that spans the ages could point to a man who doesn't age.

### Body Temperature? What Body Temperature?

Her skin is perfect, like sculpted marble and just as cool to the touch. She's unconcerned by the weather and could ski in her skivvies and still not complain. And, frankly, it's hard to cuddle up to someone with no body temperature. If you can't tempt her into the sun to warm up, perhaps her lack of body temperature indicates a lack of pulse.

### He's Always One Step Ahead of You

He can appear from nowhere to open your car door, save you from oncoming traffic, or just get the groceries inside in record time. This boy moves fast, and we're not talking about taking things to the next level on your dates. He has speedy, blink-of-an-eye responses that defy logic. Nothing in the natural world moves that quickly, though in the supernatural world it's not so uncommon.

### Really, Who Can Be *That* Perfect?

You wanted a girlfriend with all the right moves? She's got them, and then some. She moves with grace and charm, her light and sure steps never faltering. Her voice seems to charm everyone around her, lulling them into a happy and dreamy compliance. Feeling under her thrall? Chances are that you are, in fact, under a vampire's spell, but the odds are also strong that you're too blissfully happy to care.

### He Takes "Forever" Literally . . .

When he talks about being together forever, he really seems to mean it. According to this undead charmer, "till death do us part" is for losers. He's ready to commit to you until the end of time. Well, you know what your mother always said: Only a vampire can love you forever. What's a girl in love to do? Relax and enjoy yourself.

# Transformation
## A Totally Different Type of Makeover

ou're turning into something completely new, reinventing your mind, your body, and your future. Do you have any idea what to expect? Better prepare yourself; it's one wild ride. . . .

## First Things First

The most obvious change during your rebirth will be your teeth. During transformation, the canines elongate and sharpen. Try not to bite your lips—the results could be painful! Your skin will also undergo a cellular change, which is likely to result in enhanced sensitivity to UV rays. To test, find a beam of sunlight and quickly dart your toe into it. Your skin may sparkle or scorch under the light. If that happens, you'll need a dab of sunscreen before venturing out into the daylight, or you'll need to wait for overcast weather. If you're a *dhampir* (the offspring of a human and a vampire), the sun should have no effect whatsoever.

## Sensory Overload

Your physical appearance isn't the only thing that will be revamped during your transformation: Your senses will also become superacute.

### ❊ Sight

Get ready for something beyond 20/20 vision. With vamp eyesight, you will see everything near and far with perfect clarity. You'll also be able to view "waves" resonating off all living things, including plants. This energy will definitely come in handy—especially in the dark!

### ❊ Hearing

Human hearing is quite limited. As a vampire, however, your hearing will be exponentially enhanced. The initial sound wave can be quite disorienting. Prepare to eavesdrop as you never have before.

### ❊ Smell

Vampires rely on their sense of smell to assist them with tracking food and other vampires. They can distinguish a multitude of smells, often from far away. Some vampires use their sense of smell to hunt their prey—whether human, animal, or supernatural—over long distances.

### ❊ Taste

Taste and digestion are often unique to the individual vampire. While some are unable to digest mortal food and drink, others continue to enjoy the flavors and sensations of their favorite dishes and beverages. One thing is certain: All vampires are reborn with a tremendous hunger, so be prepared.

### ❊ Touch

Your sense of touch will also be refined. While you will thrill at the feeling of soft fabrics and velvety skin under your fingertips, you will recoil at anything less than fine. Perhaps it's time to invest in some beautiful gloves?

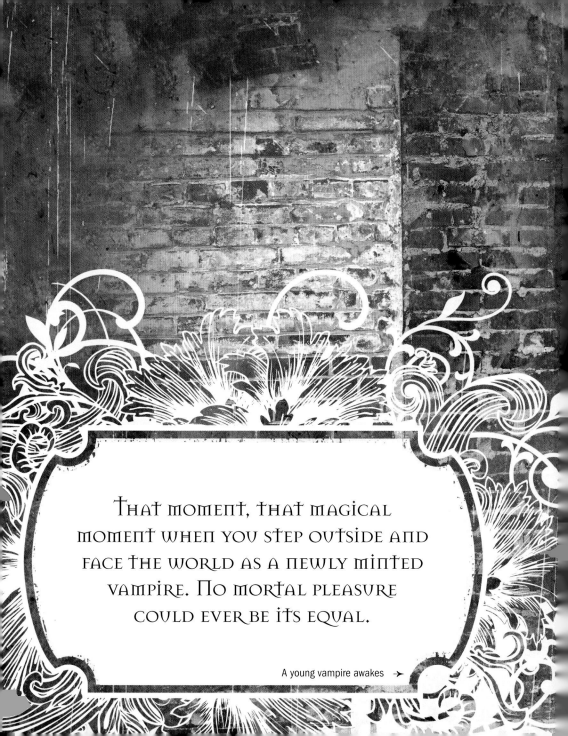

That moment, that magical moment when you step outside and face the world as a newly minted vampire. No mortal pleasure could ever be its equal.

A young vampire awakes →

# POWERS
## WHAT CAN YOU DO?

**I**t's time to exercise your new powers as a vampire. But what are they, and how do you know when you've got them? Here are some abilities that vampires are renowned for having—and some tests that will help you evaluate and tap into your strengths.

**Telepathy** The ability to communicate psychically. How to test: Focus on a willing friend, mentally project a simple statement or word, and ask them to repeat what they hear. If they successfully repeat it back, you're telepathic. If not, try this exercise with a more psychically sensitive friend. You may also find that you're able to listen in on other people's thoughts.

**Shapeshifting** The ability to transform into the animal of your choice at any time you wish. How to test: Imagine your favorite animal. Visualize the way the world looks from behind its eyes and how it feels to inhabit its body. If you can feel your body begin to change, you've got the power to shapeshift!

**Magic** The ability to cast spells and glamours. How to test: Start with a charm to see if you are able to alter memories. Can you put forward an alternative version of an event and have it be believed? Rare vampires have command of elemental magic. Can you light up a spark or make rain or fog?

### Night Vision The ability to see in the dark.

How to test: Have a friend put items in a safe test area (either outside in a place away from traffic or indoors where you will not be disturbed). Check your night vision by going to the test area at night and note which objects you see. For perfect test conditions, the area should be poorly lit but safe for your human friend.

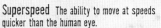

### Strength The ability to lift heavy items and exert superhuman force.

How to test: Are you superstrong? Are you continually breaking things? Test your strength with some discreet exercises: How much can you lift at the gym? How easy is it to lift your kitchen table?

### Superspeed The ability to move at speeds quicker than the human eye.

How to test: You're the sort of person who's quick on their feet. Generally all vampires have superspeed, with a few notable exceptions. But how fast can you go? Tip: If you truly have superspeed, don't bother with a stopwatch, as it will take longer to start timing than it will to get from A to B.

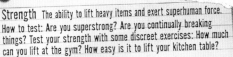

### Flight The ability to fly unaided.

How to test: No need to go leaping off buildings just yet. Do you dream of flying? Can you feel the lurch in your stomach, the weightlessness and exhilaration? Your body wants you to fly. Start off small with levitation exercises in your room. If you can suspend yourself in the air for more than five minutes or zoom down the hall, you have the power of flight.

### Healing The ability to regenerate your body on an accelerated time frame.

How to test: You never bruise or catch a cold. In fact, despite the lack of a tan, you're the picture of eerily good health. Test your regenerative abilities with a simple paper cut. How quickly do you heal?

# THE HUNT IS ON
## HOW TO FEED

Y ou've woken with a hunger that just won't quit. Nothing sates you. You're now the most dangerous creature in the world: a hungry vampire. A vampire's traditional food is human blood, the source of vitality and power. As tempting as this elixir is, responsible vampires exercise self-restraint and never completely drain a human. With a little common sense you can enjoy delicious meals that don't enrage the locals or go against your ethics. Here's how.

## HUNTING ETIQUETTE

With your enhanced senses, it's easy to track your meals. The tricky part is learning how to feed without causing a scene.

First, don't ever try to feed on a human who has been claimed by another vampire. Vampire protocol is very strict on this account. Remember what happened to James in *Twilight*? Some tender mortal may be frightfully tempting, but the goodwill and loyalty of your fellow vampires is far more important than one meal, no matter how delicious.

Second, don't enter human dwellings unless invited. This rule has its origins in long-ago superstition, and vampires from ancient bloodlines or very traditional covens may still be bound by it. Even if you discover that you can enter mortal dwellings without an invitation, it's still good manners not to break and enter.

Third, use your charm. You're a vampire, not a werewolf or a zombie (thank Nyx). You don't need to stalk and scare when so many humans already find you attractive.

## WHAT'S YOUR FLAVOR?

Some claim that certain humans give off an attractive scent, indicating sublime-tasting blood. Stand in a crowded area and sniff the air. Follow the trail, find that special someone, and ask them to dinner.

## THE SWEETEST BITE

What are your favorite pulse points? The neck, the wrist, the inner thigh? Whatever your pleasure, remember that for most humans a vampire's bite can be intense and overwhelming. You may want to use a spell or glamour to remove upsetting memories of your meal. And many caring vampires are able to use healing powers to ensure that no scars remain behind.

## DONORS

Many vampires can exist by taking small but regular blood meals from a willing donor. For some people, this generous act can be pleasurable and even form part of their relationship. The most considerate vampires listen to their donors and take only as much as they are willing to provide.

# Alternative Foods

Are you feeling spooked about drinking directly from a human? You're not the first new vampire to feel this way, and you shouldn't let your more aggressive, bloodthirsty companions mock you or pressure you into acts you're not comfortable with. For millennia, vampires have found ways to survive and thrive without harming humans. Modern vamps can enjoy a range of other options, many under the eerie fluorescent glare of your local supermarket aisle!

## Synthetic Blood

As more and more modern vampires shy away from harming humans, a shadow market has sprung up to synthesize and sell faux blood. Ask your sire or local ethical vamps, or do a little research to find synthetic blood for sale on websites that specifically cater to the undead palate.

## Animal Blood

Many who still love the thrill of the hunt find they can be satisfied by the sport of tracking nonhuman animals. With their supernatural powers, vampires can fight and feed from such formidable foes as lions, tigers, and bears. Remember to respect the endangered species list, however, and only attack animals not already under threat from mortal encroachments. And please, be discreet; a wrestling match with a leopard at the zoo might jeopardize your ability to go incognito. Feeling squeamish about grappling with a man-eater? Try sourcing animal blood from your local butcher. Pig, horse, cow, and sheep blood have none of the problems posed by stale human blood. Some vampire culinary experts even recommend mixing herbs and cereals with the fluid—such additions can make for a more satisfying bloody beverage.

## Blood Banks

Stored blood (also known as dead blood) can be fatal for some vampires and give others a bad case of indigestion. But plasma, the yellow fluid in blood, may be a more palatable option. Plasma is available from blood banks in fresh, frozen, and dehydrated varieties, making it the perfect emergency meal. Have a contact at the blood bank? See if the two of you can come to an agreement and stock up.

## Psychic Energy

Think back to your mortal days: Maybe you enjoyed being around people who were warm-hearted, happy, and passionate. They made you feel better just by being around them because they gave off high amounts of psychic or pranic energy. If you're a psi-vampire, this energy will sustain you. By aligning your chakras (energy points located throughout your body) with the chakras of another creature, you can absorb nearby energy. Go to a crowded area and open yourself up for an all-you-can-eat meal with a difference!

# GARLIC AND SILVER AND STAKES
#  OH MY!

**D**epending on your bloodline, you may have inherited certain vulnerabilities when you entered the vampire world. Read below to discover what you must avoid to survive.

### HOLY OBJECTS

Blessed water, consecrated ground, holy relics, crucifixes—traditional vampires give these objects a wide berth. An encounter with holy objects might give you a burning sensation or a strong desire to flee.

### GARLIC

A powerful antiseptic, garlic has long been used to drive away vampires in traditional folklore. However, most modern vampires have evolved resistance to this pungent herb. Unless you are extremely susceptible to its power, you may hunt in pizzerias, Chinese restaurants, and other garlicky hot spots without fear.

### WOODEN STAKES

A sharpened wedge of wood driven through the heart is fatal for most vampires. Many legends recommend specific woods like ash or hawthorn, but play it safe and don't get staked at all.

### THE SUN

The coming of the dawn is traditionally a vampire's bedtime, but what causes sure death for some vampires brings out the sparkle in others. Some vampires shimmer like diamonds when they are in the sun, others smoke and smolder, while the Rakshasa simply lose all their powers. If you're lucky, good sunglasses and a bit of sunscreen will be all you need to mix safely in the daylight world.

### Decapitation

It's the one thing that vampires, zombies, and humans have in common: None of them survive decapitation. Avoid at all costs.

### Salt

This humble ingredient is often used in protection spells due to its incorruptible nature. Throughout history, superstitious mortals have sprinkled salt around their homes and used it in exorcisms or to protect newborn babies. Ancient vampires may be vulnerable.

### Foreign Soil

For some vampires, there really is no place like home. Count Dracula could rest only when surrounded by his Romanian soil. By consecrating his imported earth, Professor Abraham Van Helsing and his companions forced Dracula out of London. You may want to keep some native earth with you to help you feel your best.

### Feng Shui

Who knew that artful placement of furniture and optimal energy flow could put a cramp in your glide? Long experienced with placating the restless *chiang-shih*, Taoist priests used feng shui to find the right burial grounds and employed mirrors and bells to combat bloodsucking spirits.

### Iron and Silver

Many vampires are repelled by these metals, noted for their purity and strength. You may find your powers are diminished in their presence, unless, of course, you are one of the rare iron-fingered vampire demons. In that case, you may laugh evilly and proceed.

### Counting Games

Some vampires love to count. In fact, they feel a compulsion to stop everything and count. Asian, Indian, South American, and European lore suggest humans leave out piles of grains, rice, poppy seeds, sand, or red peas to distract vampires from feeding. If you feel a strange desire to count small objects, you could be at risk.

# VAMPIRE TRACKERS
# THE MORTALS

Life as an immortal is not without its problems. While many humans will actively seek your embrace—and many more scoff at the possibility of your existence—a small but powerful and determined group of mortals has sworn to eradicate your kind from the planet. Who are these people, what is their problem, and what can you do about them?

## MEET YOUR MORTAL FOES

You might wonder why someone would dedicate their all-too-brief mortal life to harassing the undead. Oddly, not everyone longs for immortality. Whether hunting individually or in an organized group, these humans have made vampire research and eradication their life's mission. There are numerous cases of individuals who take arms against the vampire race. Motivated by grief or indignation, these hunters may lack supernatural skills, but make up for it with a frustrating perseverance. Often self-taught, they live a transient life, hunting vampires for profit and pride. Some even inherit the title through their family. These hunters are the easiest to overcome as their skills are inferior to their opponents'. Despite their lesser abilities, they can be dangerous in packs, and you should be wary of facing more than one human hunter.

## SCHOLARS OF THE DARKNESS

Vampire slayers are not the only cast of mortals who devote their lives to vampiric study. One group, known as vampirologists, are academics that recognize the existence of vampires and dedicate their careers to research. These humans create vampire family trees and sometimes pass down their knowledge and responsibilities to their children. One of the most famous vampire academics of all time was Professor Abraham Van Helsing. This Dutch doctor engaged in a battle of wits—and souls—with the legendary Count Dracula. Van Helsing thwarted the Count's sojourn in London and pursued him across Europe before the vampire's untimely demise. In modern times, such vampire scholars are hired by covert government departments to advise, research, and experiment with the latest in antivampire technology.

## UNDER WATCHFUL EYES

One of the more famous organized groups of vampirologists is the Watchers' Council. Called into the vocation from an early age, Watchers exist as backup to vampire slayers in a variety of ways. These polymaths train the slayers in the methods of vampire hunting, in addition to aiding them with tracking, identification, and battle strategies. They are knowledgeable about many forces of darkness, but they generally focus on vampires. Watchers are often adept at magic and fighting, but should not be considered a threat individually. That is, of course, unless the slayer they have trained is nearby and is ready to defend his scholar.

# EGALI COVEN
## ORIGIN: EGYPT

ampirologists keep meticulous records. Below is the family tree of the Egali Coven as traced by vampire expert Professor Anthony Headly-Smythe, along with his notes (in black ink). After his death, his heir picked up his studies. Her notes are in red.

This document was discovered in my ancestor's vast collection of papers, following his death by exsanguination in 1749.

**Nefer Mut (Mother of Gods)**
date unknown – 1666 AD

The original sire. It is unknown when or by whom she was turned.

**Bastet**
Servant of Nefer Mut
3415 BC

Killed by Roman vampire hunter Silvrius, a dhampir.

**Scipio Laelius**
Soldier
47 BC–1666 AD

Moved to Rome to escape suspicion?

**Hanisa**
Hun maiden
70–166 AD

**Phaedra**
Failed oracle
219–249 AD

Possible case of vampire suicide

**Theodora**
A great beauty
367–976 AD

**Rosamund**
Coven princess
448–1666 AD

Aulus Africanus
Soldier
36–15 BC
Also killed by
Silvius.

Gaius Asiaticus
Soldier
39 BC–16 AD

Quintas Flavius Nobilior
Soldier
41 BC–893 AD

Alaric
Visigoth leader & warrior
148–1666 AD

Bero
Hun, known as
"the Skinner"
228–893 AD

Sabine
The Cathar
1159–1666 AD???

Abelard
369–1076 AD
Not, of course, the
famed philosopher!

Piers of Sussex
aka Piers the Pardoner
1079–1326 AD

Oswin of Bath
A sapper
1442–1666 AD
Aha! So is this
when they moved
to London?

Did Sabine
survive the fire?
Tantalizing signs
point to yes.

It would appear that the Great Fire
of London in 1666 claimed the lives
of Rosamund, Alaric, and Oswin of
Bath.... Some covens are renowned
for "firing" fallen vampires—did
this ritual start with the Great
Fire of London?

Did a rival coven set the Great
Fire of London to kill members
of the Egli coven and diminish
its strength? A most intriguing
possibility . . .

Siring rights:
The coven seems to have dictated which
members could sire. The soldier Scipio Laelius
appears to be the main sire—did Nefer Mut
choose the females? Possible ritual involved.
Numbers were kept to four women, four men.

# Supernatural Foes

nfortunately, vampires are not always at the top of the food chain. There are a slew of beasts, humanoids, and not-so-divine creatures who can threaten your precious immortality. Here are some to watch out for.

## Other Vampires

Sadly, the biggest threat to vampires is often other vampires. Petty squabbles, vendettas, and factional strife frequently result in vampire-on-vampire violence. Some especially nasty vamps become trackers and hunt down their bloodsucking brethren.

## Dhampirs

The offspring of a vampire father and a human mother, the *dhampir* has all the vampire strengths but none of the weaknesses. With their gift for identifying vampires, *dhampirs* act as hunters for hire.

## Daywalkers

Exhibiting all the strengths of *dhampirs*, daywalkers are created when vampires bite pregnant mothers, transforming their unborn children in utero. Daywalkers have a powerful hatred of vampires and are dedicated to eradicating them.

## Slayers

Slayers, females with enhanced fighting and healing powers, are mystically called into action. They generally hunt alone, though there are cases of a slayer surrounding herself with friends and helpers.

78904568
NEW ORLEANS, LA
PARISH POLICE

6'

5'

90749203
SUNNYDALE, CA POLICE DEPT

### WEREWOLVES

There are tales of bloody werewolf–vamp feuds continuing through history, though some vampire covens have made treaties with werewolf packs.

### DEMONS

Considered the pure form of vampirism untainted by human essence, demons can be deadly foes, as they have greater power than vampires and can kill them easily.

### WITCHES

Dark or light, it doesn't matter; witches present a real threat to vampires. They can severely incapacitate a vampire through curses, raise demons, or cast the ultimate spell: resouling.

### ZOMBIES

Given their putrefied state, zombies make for unsuitable vampire meals. Despite their undead status, vampires are susceptible to zombie attacks as well as zombie viruses.

666000666
WALPURGISNACHT COUNTY PUBLIC SAFETY

75490267
SALEM, MA POLICE DEPT

ZZZ890ZZZ
YONKERS, NY HOMELAND SECURITY

Never underestimate the cleverness of mortals. They are beasts, but deadly ones.

← Staking scene from *Salem's Lot* (2004)

# WELCOME TO THE
# FAMILY

Immortality is a long time to go it alone. Seeking protection, hunting partners, or simple companionship, many vampires choose to live with their brethren and form clans, houses, or covens. It's like a family, with all the love and bickering that the word suggests. For newborn vampires, family can be especially important. Older, more established vampires can help with your training and education. Many older vampires, in fact, find it satisfying to take a new vampire under their wing. Your family may contain mentors to help you develop your newfound abilities. Plus, without a family's protection and guidance, a fledgling may take unnecessary risks and be exposed to angry humans, vampire hunters, or worse. So what's your ideal coven? At right, some models to consider.

## NOMADS

Ever dreamed of backpacking with friends on an extended vacation? Perhaps you're a nomad. Traveling from city to city, informal wandering families never stay in the same place for long. If you yearn for travel and adventure, this is the coven for you.

## VEGETARIAN

Eschewing human blood, many covens live off the blood of animals. Some such covens are steadfastly pacifist, refusing to take part in any interspecies or vampire wars. In comparison, other families will actively battle other vampires if the need arises but prefer to make truces. Often reflective and family-oriented, these covens are great centers of support for vampires.

## DARK AND DANGEROUS

Maybe you have a hankering for a traditional coven and its plots, battles, and dark thirst for humanity. In her Vampire Chronicles, Anne Rice revealed the gruesome secrets of one such group. The vampire Armand led a Parisian coven under a cemetery that fed off Paris for years, killing mortals and vampires alike. If you join a dark coven, be wary of falling behind the times. Armand killed off most of his cult after the vampire Lestat ridiculed them for their outmoded ways.

## ANCIENT ARISTOCRACY

Do you consider yourself above others? Are you supernaturally gifted? Do you have a yen to bend others to your will? If your vampire brethren tease you for your regal ways, you may be suitable for coronation! A handful of vampire families are considered vampire royalty and are the arbiters and enforcers of the bloodied world. With some more than 3,000 years old, membership in these covens is strictly by invitation only.

## RABID RAVERS

You can still be the life of the party even if you're dead: Seek out and join one of the many covens of nightclubbing superbrats with bite. Take Deacon Frost's gang from *Blade* as an example. Part of the House of Erebus, Frost's coven is filled with hard-partying vamps who work to fulfill their leader's plans. When they're not hosting warehouse rave "blood baths," they're plotting to rule the world.

## THE LONER

If you're the type who prefers your own company, why bother with a coven? Take to the open road by yourself and have an adventure. You will always meet people (not, um, just your meals), and you'll never have to endure clashes about where to go or what to see or any of the usual family drama.

# HOW TO FORM
# Your · Own · Coven

oining an existing coven can be difficult, especially if you're trying to forge a bond with vampires who have known each other for centuries. Some covens may have a reputation for snobbery against newborn vampires. Others may have waiting lists of several centuries. If you've looked around and haven't found a good match, perhaps it's time to create your own. Here's how.

## Define Your Belief system and Purpose

What does your coven stand for? Some covens are supportive and spiritual, others devoted to darkness. A solid foundation will help bring members together and keep them loyal. A good place to start is by defining your basic beliefs about the origin of vampires and their place in the world. Consider your feeding and hunting preferences as well as any special skills or interests that will help define your group.

## Decide on Your Structure

Will your coven be democratic? Or will it have one supreme master? How and where will you meet? Existing covens have a wide range of organizational styles. Which speaks to you and to the types of vampires you hope will join you? And because any group of vampires will sometimes disagree, you'll want to have a basic set of rules for behavior, for decision-making, and for entering and leaving the coven.

## Admit New Members

Will membership in your coven be a closely guarded prize? Or will you welcome anyone who wants to join? Decide how you'll admit new members to your group. Some covens have different levels or stages that new vampires progress through until they are full-fledged members with complete privileges. Let prospective members have a trial period when they can get to know the group and its workings before either one of you commits. Whenever you do admit new vampires, welcome them with an initiation ceremony.

## Vet Your Members

Beyond defining your membership guidelines, you may also choose to seek out vampires who have special, and useful, talents. For instance, a vampire gifted with charisma can harmonize the coven's mood at intense moments, and every coven needs a strong hunter to help find new hunting grounds and refine techniques.

## Develop Rituals

Traditions and rituals deepen the bond between coven members and can also be an opportunity for vampires to enhance their spiritual or magical practices. Whether it's the full moon, a member's initiation, or maybe even the release of the latest vampire movie, decide what events are important and how you'll celebrate them.

# LIVING THE UNDEAD LIFESTYLE

## WHEREIN THE SECRETS OF VAMPIRE STYLE ARE REVEALED

**Y**ou've been turned. There is no going back to your mundane former life, when mortal blood coursed through your veins, sunlight beat on your face, and eternity was only a dream.

Rejoice: Life in dark majesty awaits. It is time for you to discover your timeless identity and to make a look of your own from the vast range of vampiric fashion, makeup, and hairstyles.

Learn, gentle reader, how you can transform the most basic of lodgings into a seductive lair of pleasure and repose, as well as how to throw parties that will be talked about through the ages. And with your enhanced hearing, you deserve fitting music.

But what of your life outside the crypt? How will you spend your confined days and boundless nights? And how will you maintain relations with people unkissed by the night? Fear not, for detailed instructions follow.

# COMING OUT
## OF THE CRYPT

ife for you has changed irrevocably. This will be noticed by your family and friends: a change in the hours you keep, your diet, and your very essence. You will eventually have to tell them that you are a vampire. This will be a conversation fraught with emotion. They will certainly fear for you and for themselves—as the odds are great that they have not come across a vampire before—and they will surely have questions. Here's how to handle your dark debut.

Do choose a quiet and relaxed time to disclose your news to others. Good time: at home after a nice meal (made by and not of humans). Bad time: at Uncle Don's wedding.

Don't snack while you tell them. Emotional eating is bad at any time, but in this scenario it's not going to help anyone.

Do talk in a calm voice. People will get scared if you shout or call others names. Be composed and collected, like Gandhi. You know, if Gandhi were a vampire.

Don't show off all your new powers. Your nearest and dearest will get used to them soon enough. Right now, they just need to get used to you as a vampire. Not a vampire who can fly/transform/suddenly perform martial arts. Give them time.

Do share stories about vampires you really like, so your friends and family can get to know your role models and learn more about vampirism in the process. Your parents will take heart in your having new friends—especially if your new pals seem to be upstanding and not likely to, you know, feast off your family.

Don't try to turn those closest to you into vampires. At least not yet. You have an eternity in which to make these important decisions—and don't forget, your friends and family should get some say in the matter, just as you did.

Do warm your hands prior to having the discussion. Your mom will want to hold your hand, and the shock of your marble skin might make her cry.

Don't use your powers of persuasion. Your loved ones need to process this new information without any influence. Otherwise, you'll never feel quite comfortable with their acceptance.

Do answer all their questions truthfully. If you're going to share the ultimate truth about yourself, it's best to be completely open about everything—except what you did last summer, because nothing good can come from that.

Don't assume you will be rejected. You were given a chance to grow into a vampire; give those around you the chance to grow into more accepting mortals.

# How to Look the Part

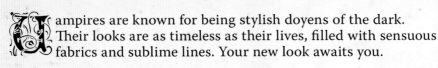

ampires are known for being stylish doyens of the dark. Their looks are as timeless as their lives, filled with sensuous fabrics and sublime lines. Your new look awaits you.

Let your hair color reflect your bloodthirsty personality. Bleach out some streaks and dye vivid red stripes.

Wear the signs of your coven for pride and to let other vamps know who you are.

Capes are so last millennium. A stylish long jacket gets the job done with flair. Bonus—pockets!

Wristbands cover up your lack of a pulse.

Capelets give all the drama of a cape with a sassy modern touch.

A large necklace deflects those pesky wooden stakes that can really ruin your day.

Worried that your icy touch will give you away as a member of the undead? Just don a pair of gloves!

A vamp may need to run on a moment's notice. Be sure your boots are functional as well as stylish.

# Traditional
## GET THE LOOK
## TO DIE FOR

The traditional vampire look is moored in Victorian- and Georgian-era mourning dress. Filled with flourishes and melodrama, this style hearkens back to a time when clothing was one of the few socially acceptable ways people could publicly show emotion—which is perfect for the life of stoic secrecy that awaits you.

### Fashion for Him

The traditional vampire look for males is one of excess, luxury, and decadence—you're not the type of vampire to hide yourself, and you know how to make an entrance.

This look favors crisp white shirts. Seek out the frill and flounce of ruffled shirts, and use a simple cravat or formal tie (preferably black or a nice bloodred) to complement. Informal or overly casual clothes will detract from the overall look.

Go long with your coats. While a frock coat lacks the moody drama of a cape, it is a flattering line that lends an air of power and ritual. Plus, coats have pockets, which can come in handy because—really—even if you do have an eternity, you don't want to spend all of it retracing your steps to find your misplaced wallet.

When it comes to footwear, your shoes should be refined. Count Dracula is the embodiment of aristocracy and would never wear sneakers or motorcycle boots. Try black leather dress boots, sleek patent-leather tuxedo shoes, or a spats boot.

Run riot with accessories: gold- or silver-topped canes, fob watches, tie pins, fingerless gloves. The right accessories can, if properly weighted, give incredible authority to your outfit.

Experiment with different bodices, skirt lengths, and boot heights for the look that best suits you.

Speaking of boots, they're the best choice of footwear for you. A slight heel gives calf definition and will tie in with your femme look. Seek more feminine boots with dainty buckles, buttons, and laces.

As a female vampire, you are not constrained like men when it comes to color. Experiment with rich, indulgent hues and brocades for a sumptuous look. Silks, taffeta, satins, and lace can be any shade, but rich bloodreds will help your cold skin come alive. As for hair, sleek chignons and soft curls are the best coiffures for the elegant lady vampire; messy, deconstructed buns and ponytails (tied with a satin ribbon to the side) can show your lustful side. Go elegantly crazy with costume jewelry: Beautiful crystals across your former pulse points (neck and wrists) will help you glow.

Taking the time to dress with beautiful fabrics and dramatic shapes is the hallmark of a vampire. Rituals of luxury often make people feel happier and more confident about their appearance. And if you feel happy and confident, the world will literally fall at your feet.

## Fashion for Her

The traditional look for girls is feminine and seductive. Victorian-inspired mourning clothes put particular emphasis on a small waist. If you don't breathe, achieving the look won't trouble you in the slightest. If you still do breathe, consider it practice for later, because the traditional lady-vamp look is big on corsets.

Of course, you don't have to wear a corset. Even a belt or a sash will suffice. When dressing, consider yourself a silhouette: a cinched waist with volume above and below. The classic vampire aesthetic for women can be quite flattering, allowing you to layer where you please and dress to your unnatural strengths.

# Eternal Beauty

## is in the eye of the beholder

Whether you want to look damned good or just damned, glamorous vampire style isn't hard to attain. Complex and dramatic in appearance, this distinctive look evokes sirens of the silver screen and their dashing consorts, with a modern gothic twist. The emphasis is high-contrast, black-and-white melodrama.

## Hair

You can toy with your hairstyle to express your varying levels of hunger and comfort. Well-groomed, conditioned hair lets everyone know you're on top of the food chain. For a wilder look, ladies can back-brush and scrunch before pinning into an updo; guys can tousle and use pomade to enhance and add texture.

## Skin

Brush on rice powder for silky smooth skin. For those going for the *Twilight* sparkle, use an ultra-pale loose glitter powder that shimmers in the sun. For defined cheeks, trace and blend black eye shadow from just under your cheekbone, but don't overdo it. Subtly blended, this can chisel those cheeks into deathly taut perfection.

## Lips

Nothing is a better indicator of your hunger than your lips. Feeling full? A luscious red gloss will let the civilians know you're sated and safe. Want to announce your hunger? Wash out your lips with foundation or a skin-tone lipstick, preferably matte, to signal your bloody dehydration.

## Eyes

The eyes are your greatest weapon, enticing sires and prey alike. Use liquid eyeliner to paint long, languorous lines across your lids for full seductive power. Go for a dark and subtly shimmery metallic eye shadow in black, blue, or even purple. A touch of red eye shadow or eyeliner along the bottom eyelids will show your restless hunger. Style brows into a devilish, witty arch.

## Contacts

For the budget-unconscious, cool contact lenses are a great way to get immediate impact. Red contacts will definitely lend an overpowering demonic appearance. Want intensity? Try pure black. Light contacts or vivid blues and greens will also make your eyes stand out, whatever your skin tone.

# Demonic
## A clawed vamp aesthetic

 ore hellish outcast than refined count, the demonic vampire is a crazed beast. There is no shadow deep enough to hide his or her fire: Everything about this look is extreme, shocking, and sure to scare small children.

### Dressing Down

Practical and aggressive, demonic vampires are not known for sartorial excess. Their look is the result of continual battle and feeding. Clothing is utilitarian, without ornamentation, and often damaged from previous fights.

### Basic Boy Demon

The classic uniform for a demonic vampire male is a pair of well-worn leather pants and a waistcoat. They're practical, hard-wearing, and hide a multitude of sins. Thick, hard, buckled boots give added height and support for those long hours standing as Hell's sentry.

### Fashionista from Hell

The female of this deadly species may borrow this manly style or go for a look that's more she-demon. Shredded and layered black dresses can show the chaos and power you wield. Team layers of black netting for a demonic tutu, with ripped stockings and battered army boots. If you're more batlike than human, consider fashioning wings from wire and flesh-colored hosiery—stain the fabric with tea, dirt, and the odd splash of red ink as a display of battles past.

### Style for the Unturned

The demonic look can demand physical commitment. If you've not yet turned, try on some of the less over-the-top options for size. Hair can be shaved off or buzz-cut to give the look of a battle-ready beast. Alternatively, long, wild hair can give that frighteningly feral look. Contact lenses in deep red, cat's-eye yellow, or ice blue give an intense but easily removable look. Until you grow actual talons or claws, grow your nails long and file them into sharp points to show your otherworldly nature.

### Accessories of Evil

The true demon may have horns and long, sharp fangs. While some aspiring vamps go so far as to have permanent horns implanted in their heads and undergo surgery for fangs that last forever, these affectations will be pointless once you are actually turned. Instead, try stylish horns that stick on with spirit gum, and subtle but scary temporary fangs. Those who are even more dedicated to the demonic look may be drawn to tattoos and piercings. Just remember, eternity is an awfully long time to be stuck with a tattoo you no longer like. Think about less permanent ways to show your allegiance to the dark side.

**F**amed for their agility and fitness, these vampires focus on the exquisite art of fighting. Acting either individually or as part of an army, they live for the battle and honor their code. This style is all about ease of movement and camouflage, not fashion. The soldier is concerned not with the catwalk, merely with the next fight. Clothing is his second skin: Apparel must make it easy to run, perform martial arts, and defy the laws of physics.

## The Darker Side of Style

For creatures who fight in perpetual darkness, black is the color of choice. This isn't your traditional tuxedo-shirt–style vamp look. A dark, monochromatic palette reinforces your formidable warrior status and makes you appear truly intimidating to mortals and werewolves alike. Impressive jet-black sunglasses are a must as your trademark accessory. Day or night, they will make you inscrutable.

## Crowning Glory

Your hair, preferably jet black like your outfit, should be slicked back into a tight braid or cut short for easy maintenance; you're more committed to the fight than to your 'do. A buzz cut says "military efficiency" for the male or female vamp, although more image-conscious fighters may prefer a short, easy-to-care-for bob.

## Elements of Street Style

You're in the vampire special forces. Think flak jackets and body armor buckled at different angles with pockets and loops full of metal-plated gadgets. If you're feeling the chill, invest in a dramatic long leather coat. Go for a red lining on the coat's inside to stun your foes. Long leather pants are durable and stylish at the same time.

## High and Tight

For the lethal femmes fatales, it's going to be a tight fit. Vamp soldiers like Selene from *Underworld* favor formfitting black leather, rubber, and PVC. For the all-in-one look, start with a basic catsuit and accessorize on top with holsters, thick leather-looking corsets, extra belts, and wrist cuffs. Knee-high boots with heels can be your friend—the height will give great definition to your legs. If you're not confident with heels, wear them around the crypt for a while and practice some tumbles to make sure that you can take on anything while still looking fabulous.

## Fight to Unite

Remember: These vampires are in peak physical condition, so keep up your fitness regimen to feel more confident and healthy. Studying martial arts will also make you more attractive as a potential recruit.

# THINK · OUTSIDE · THE · COFFIN

If you're still searching for your perfect look, try on one of these other, lesser-known vampire styles. And even if you're a diehard traditional sort, there's always Halloween.

## HARAJUKU VAMPIRE

Cutie-pies with fangs, these little munchkins coquettishly style themselves like the boys and girls of Yoyogi Park in Tokyo, but with a little undead flair. To get the look, load up your hair with gel, and form triangles to achieve an anime effect—dyed or peroxided hair looks especially fierce. For boy vamps, try dramatic capes or frock coats, buckled trousers, and ruffled white shirts with turned-up collars; add a loose red tie to complete the outfit. To femme it up, go for amped platform shoes, teeny tartan skirts, white knee-high socks, and cute blouses. And if you want to become a totally *kawaii* killer, finish by accessorizing your outfit with different-colored contact lenses and a pair of plush rabbit ears.

## Egyptian Vampire

One for the exhibitionist vampire, all this look requires is some deftly wrought precious metal and judicious use of flowing purple, the color of royalty. Oh, and bucketloads of confidence. Queen Akasha popularized the style and sashayed into eternity wearing only a belt, a bra, and a headdress of glittering wealth, along with some flowing drapes for modesty. Unless you have ready access to bras made from precious metal, a fitted sleeveless dress in white or purple shows Egyptian flair. Accessories are key with this look: enameled bangles, belts, rings, and necklaces. Straightened hair is best—top it off with a headdress or beaded headpiece. Use thick eyeliner to give yourself Egyptian eyes and matte brown lipstick to show your dust-kissed pout. For the guys, a ceremonial skirt, decorated armbands, and pharaoh-style headdress is all that is required. If you're a shy guy, a cotton tunic is the perfect base for the look, which you can then accessorize with basic sandals, collar, and metal cuffs.

## Retro '80s Vampire

Defined by Catherine Deneuve and David Bowie in the 1983 film *The Hunger*, this style can jump from sculpted leather couture to refined elegance. Sharp suits for both men and women take these vampires far above their base brethren, raising them to heavenly art forms. During the day, expensive, beautifully tailored clothing shows your (very) old money appeal. At night, dress up to go clubbing. Boys go glam in black satin shirts, pointed boots, and leather pants, while the girls spice it up with sculpted leather jackets, tight black dresses, fascinators, angled sunglasses, and chainmail gloves. Don't forget an ankh around your neck.

## Punk Vampire

If vampires are the ultimate bad boys and girls, punk vampires are the ultimate bloodsuckers. Their clothes are studded, ripped, zipped, and fastened with pins and chains. With colorful mohawks and asymmetrical bobs, punk vampires are fanatical for piercings, tattoos, and striking makeup. This vampire style also incorporates the goth and surf punk subgenres. Go for a rough-trade, wild-child look with ripped denim, black leather vests, army surplus boots, fishnet stockings (for boys and girls!), and a shirt that looks like it was ripped off Sid Vicious. The key item for this look is the leather jacket—the older the vampire, the older and greater the jacket's history. Did yours come from the back of a slayer? Does it carry a million tears and repairs? As for accessories, remember, your outfit can never have enough buckles and you can never have enough cheap metal jewelry. Girls may want to hunt through thrift stores for vintage cocktail or prom dresses—the more beat up, the better!

# CHOOSING YOUR
# VAMPIRE NAME

Many vampires like to rename themselves after they've changed to mark the beginning of their new lives. Often these new names are chosen to reflect a coven or personal philosophy, or are given to vampires based on their abilities.

## THE RENAMING RITUAL

It's no surprise that the most famous vampire names are from Eastern Europe, home to the infamous Count Dracula and the region where the vampire legend rose from the shadows. In fact, the word *vampire* (*upir*) has roots in all Slavic and Turkish languages. But don't let this limit you, and

likewise don't let your lack of a centuries-old birth certificate keep you from dropping in a Count, Contessa, Lord, or other royal title for a regal touch. Don't worry—after a few decades (mere seconds for you), no one will remember when you weren't royalty. The document at the right lists intriguing options for both titles and surnames.

## Titles for Men

Baron  *Czech for baron*
Dominus  *Latin for lord*
Greve  *Swedish for count*
Imperator  *Latin for emperor*
Marquis  *or, for Spanish flair,* Marquéz
Landgrave  *a lordly German title*
Chevalier  *French for knight*

## Titles for Women

Baronka  *Czech for baroness*
Domina  *Latin for lady*
Grevinna  *Swedish for countess*
Imperatrix  *Latin for empress*
Marquise  *or, for Spanish flair,* Marquesa
Principessa  *Italian princess*
Bantiarna  *Irish countess*

## Names for Men

Crnobog  *"black god," the Slavic god of evil and darkness*
Drogo  *ghost*
Herkus  *home ruler*
Ivan  *variant of John, made famous by Ivan the Terrible*
Marko  *warlike*
Nikolai  *victory of the people*
Perun  *slavic god of lightning, his name means "thunder"*
Veles/Volos  *slavic god of the underworld, known for magic and trickery*
Vlad/Vladimir  *rules the world*
Vodnik  *slavic spirit*

## Names for Women

Aleria  *eagle*
Anastasia  *resurrection*
Ashskhen  *elegant*
Elodia  *fortune*
Fiona  *pale and beautiful*
Marishka  *sea of bitterness*
Narcisa  *sleep*
Roze  *Lithuanian for rose*
Tatiana  *precious, from a beautiful land*
Zofie  *wisdom (perfect for the head of a coven)*
Zsizsi  *nickname for rumored vampire Countess Erzsébet Báthory*

## INFAMOUS INDICATORS

Until you become a vampire supermodel, you'll need a last name. Perhaps you belong to an established order or coven and can take its name as your own. Many covens acquire a family surname based on the leader's former family name, such as Cullen, Boiroi, or Torok. If you belong to such a coven, take your leader's surname to show your allegiance. Older and aristocratic covens, particularly European groups founded in medieval times, use the leader's place of origin for their surname (Saint-Clair, d'Aquitaine, and di Pisa, for example). (Some, however, have modernized their names to avoid hunters.) Some vampires have been given nicknames based on their terrible strengths and cruelties. For instance, the Romanian prince Dracula was known as Vlad the Impaler because of his love of impaling his victims. William the Bloody maintains that his name originates from his love of bloodshed, though others point instead to his "bloody awful" poetry.

# Vampire Etiquette

tiquette is a collection of rules and behaviors that form the basis of good decorum. From table manners to the perfect greeting and handshake, etiquette helps vampires glide through eternal life with ease and without embarrassment.

## Gracious Elements

It is a little-known fact that vampires are sticklers for etiquette. Far from the lawless blood-sprayers of myth, many strive to comport themselves with a beauty that pleases all. The most suave are aware that while etiquette can vary between cultures, the true diplomat takes time to learn the differences; a polite handshake in Norway may be considered an insult in another country. Thus, a vampire of true distinction roams the world with good grace and behavior. By avoiding faux pas, the vampire can also avoid unwittingly insulting another vampire, which could result in centuries of conflict with the offended.

## Basic Courtesy when Interacting with Mortals

While in the mortal realm, it is easy to remember mortal frailties. Once you have been turned, however, you may need a bit of reminding to recall what those mysterious mortals need. For instance, when greeting humans, remember to warm your hands beforehand or wear gloves—the shock of cold skin is inconsiderate. Humans need warmth: Remember to use heaters in the car or home to ensure their comfort. When walking with a human, keep to the right. As the stronger person, you are best equipped to push aside any threat to them (people, out-of-control cars, and so on).

## Entertaining Humans

Mortal guests add a certain . . . something to any vampire dinner party. Do remember, when you deign to attend a human dinner party, to BYOB (bring your own blood). This will make other guests feel relaxed and help you stave off temptation. If another vamp is hosting the party, be sure to have tidy table manners when drinking from a donor (a guest that has generously offered to slake your thirst during the festivities). This care will reduce blood stains and ensure that you're invited again. Finally, send thank-you notes to the donors after the dinner party.

## How to Behave with Other Vampires

When meeting with an older vampire or a coven leader, do not reach out to shake hands. Instead, bow or curtsy in respect. (This may not apply to modern coven heads in the United States.) Vampire dinner parties require you to bring a present for the host. Remember to dress up your donor with a red bow. It's only right to offer the neck to another vampire if you're about to share a meal. Thank-you notes are a must, but remember that traditional manners say that it's rude to write letters in red. That's right, no more letters in blood. Finally, know that declining a meal with a vampire is an egregious insult and thus may set things aflame—most likely you.

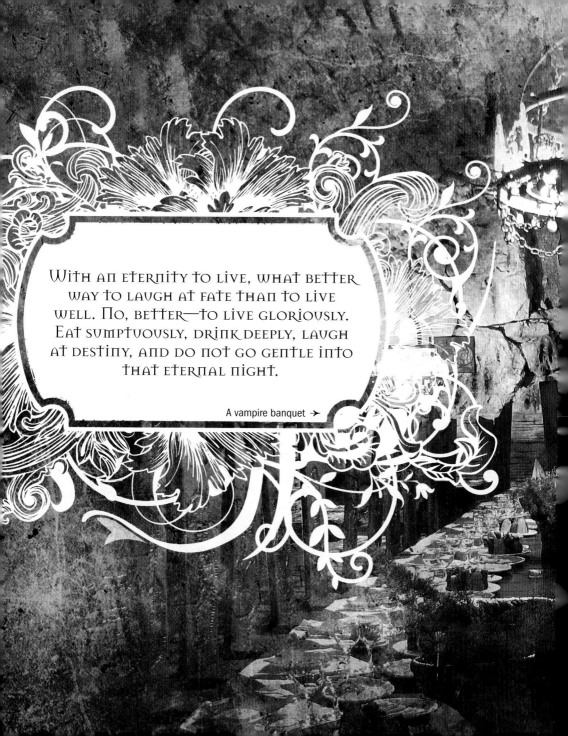

With an eternity to live, what better way to laugh at fate than to live well. No, better—to live gloriously. Eat sumptuously, drink deeply, laugh at destiny, and do not go gentle into that eternal night.

A vampire banquet →

# Finishing You Off

An uneducated vampire doesn't last long in the world, and that's why many newly turned vamps are whisked off to vampire academies for intensive training. Created by aristocratic vamps to educate their fledgling covens, these nocturnal finishing schools have since opened their doors to other newcomers, training vampires who are taking their first faltering steps toward true accomplishment.

Student vampires spend a year learning basics like hunting, feeding, deportment, diplomacy, languages, and safety. Then, in their final three years, they specialize in more advanced subjects for which they show either a gift or an interest.

If you are unable to attend a vampire finishing school, take heart. By studying the topics at right, you are well on the path to becoming a truly accomplished vampire. Who knows? Your self-improvement efforts may even attract the attention of a coven.

Mr. Miller is a psycho!

Good times at the graveyard

# ST. VLADIMIR'S SECONDARY SCHOOL

# **REPORT CARD**

**STUDENT NAME:** _Isolde Garibaldi_  **COVEN:** _Garibaldi_  **YEAR:** _3_  **AGE:** _217 Years_

_Walpurgisnacht_ **TERM: 18**_32_

| SUBJECT | PROFESSOR | MARKS IN TERM (MAX 100%) | MARKS IN EXAM (MAX 100%) | REMARKS |
|---|---|---|---|---|
| Diplomacy | Dulcelang | 91% | 21% | Scores highly in mesmerism. Showed ill humor in Socratic discourse exam, branding Professor Lorenzo "an egregiously dim and foul tuber" after failing to secure negotiation. |
| Curses | Execrato | 100% | 100% | Isolde's cursing abilities are uncharted and profound. Routinely leaves first-year test subjects in tears. Excellent. |
| Language: Romany | Vlax | 92% | 93% | Hypnotic enunciation but could do better with greater effort. Has shown aptitude for insults not seen since Eckhardt the Irascible. Outstanding. |
| Advanced Defense | Shen-chi | 62% | 71% | Would learn more techniques were she quiet during practice sessions. |
| Advanced Hunting | Dasharatha | 64% | 68% | Continually attends class without required hunting equipment and uniform. |
| Music | Sirena | 76% | absent | Could do better with more practice. Did not attend exam. |

# VAMPITECHTURAL DIGEST
# WHAT'S YOUR STYLE?

Once you've graduated from vampire finishing school, you'll need a place to call your own, and to furnish it in a style that reflects the immortal you. Some emerging vamps have found ways to integrate their style into any environment, even one shared with finicky mortals, such as parents or roommates. How will you make that space your own? Here are some questions to get you started.

## WHEN YOUR NOCTURNAL PROWL IS DONE, YOU LIE DOWN TO SLEEP

A. On a high-tech pod that blocks out those obnoxious UV rays.
B. On a sumptuous bed made with luxurious, soft velvet.
C. Wherever you can that's dark: a cave or crypt in the cemetery.
D. On a couch that you found on the side of the road.

## WHEN IT COMES TO ART, YOU PREFER

A. Abstract paintings and black-and-white photography.
B. Grand-scale paintings from the great European masters.
C. Cave paintings.
D. Out-of-date calendars.

## YOU LIKE TO RELAX BY

A. Going out to a rave and mixing it up.
B. Taking in your favorite opera from your private box.
C. There is no relaxing, only moving on to the next place.
D. Just hanging out with friends and laughing—shouldn't be too fancy.

## YOUR ROOM HAS A FIREPLACE. YOU DECORATE IT WITH

A. Nothing. You prefer clear spaces and hate clutter.
B. Heaps of fine silver candlesticks and mementos from times past.
C. You travel light—there's nothing to put on the mantel.
D. Improvised candlesticks from bottles and interesting objects that you found in vacant lots.

## CLEANLINESS IS

A. Essential—messiness shows a messy mind.
B. Something that you leave to the servants to maintain.
C. Something you never think about.
D. You try to clean but always get distracted by TV.

## YOUR PERSONALITY SUMMED UP IN TWO WORDS IS

A. Powerful, intimidating.
B. Reflective, wise.
C. Compulsive, paranoid.
D. Impulsive, disorganized.

## MOSTLY A'S:
## YOUR STYLE IS MODERN MINIMALIST

If it's bright, shiny, and high-tech, you must have it. Your modern style shows in your cool and detached personality. Spaces must be clear of distraction and have only the essentials. Your car is sleek and swift, your wardrobe is the definition of understated elegance, and your personal space is so cool it's chilly.

## MOSTLY B'S: YOUR STYLE IS GOTHIC GRANDEUR

You were old school before school even started. Traditional and dramatic, you embrace the proud history of vampdom and prefer the finer things in life. Anything that is old and mysterious speaks to you.

## MOSTLY C'S:
## YOUR STYLE IS TRANSIENT

Unpredictable and dangerous, you are always on the move. Your wandering ways testify to your independence and refusal to bond with people, places, or objects. Your style is that you live without style—you are pure hunter— and where you lay your head is of little importance to you. As long as it's out of the sunlight, that is.

## MOSTLY D'S: YOUR STYLE IS BASEMENT DWELLER

You're a jumble of contradictions and it shows in your home. You're all about living in the moment, and despite great dreams, you never plan ahead. You Dumpster-dive for furniture, and your lack of money makes you great at improvised home decoration.

# YOUR VAMPIRE ROOM

lair is more than a place to relax after a night's hunt, unharmed by the scathing sun; it should also be an expression of your personality. Be inspired by this decadent lesson in interior design.

Stencils can go any-where—walls, ceiling, even furniture.

Candlelight sets the mood for night-dwelling vamps.

Even sleepless ones appreciate luxurious bedclothes.

Paint walls to change the mood. Try walls in different colors.

Hang scarves to add mood and color without great expense.

Heavy velvet curtains are a must to keep out those deadly rays.

Refinish furniture for a lived-in look.

Drape tiebacks can add a touch of glamour.

Ceiling-mounted bed canopy = major drama.

Throw pillows transform a bed, couch, or chair.

# Ghoulish Gardens

It's not all about crypts. Some vampires enjoy a beautiful garden at night, where they can use their olfactory sense to sniff out blooming beauties. The aim with any night garden is to select plants that release their full beauty in darkness.

## Night Bloomers

Some flowers open and release their scent at night. Go for high-visibility flowers, preferably white, which will make them easier to appreciate in the darkness.

**Jasmine**  At night when the air is hot, this flower is almost as seductive as you. These small white flowers release a nearly overwhelming scent that indulges the senses.

**Cereus**  A night-flowering cactus, cereus produces incredibly intense flowers of sharp, symmetrical petals. Dazzlingly complex, these cacti can also be used as houseplants.

**Tobacco**  You heard right: The main ingredient in cigarettes is also one of the biggest and most beautiful night bloomers. Let *Nicotiana tabacum* stand tall, and its creamy trumpet flowers will open at night with a sweet perfume that smells beautiful (unlike cigarettes, which will disgust your finely tuned sense of smell).

## Carnivorous Plants

Plants that bite the hand that feeds them, carnivorous plants are botanical soul mates to vampires. Fascinating in their appearance, they are natural insect killers. Renfield, Dracula's insect-obsessed and demented minion, would either really love them or resent the intrusion into his food source.

**Cape Sundew**  With long sticky tendrils reaching out for food, the Cape sundew is utterly fascinating to behold as it curls around an insect. Easy to grow, this member of the *Drosera* family actually liquefies its prey.

**Sarracenia**  Pitcher plants in the *Sarracenia* genus entice insects with rich nectar before drowning and eating them. *Sarracenia* are striking when grown in groups—their tall, flowering tubes resemble irises.

**Venus Flytrap**  This plant has some deadly moves. It waits, lobes open, for juicy flies and spiders to trip its trigger hairs, then—snap!—it closes to devour its prey. These supercharged moves make the Venus flytrap the supreme hunter of the normally sedate plant world.

## Black Flowers

Finally, a flower to match your soul. They may be a little harder to see at night, but black flowers bring high-contrast drama to your garden. Some to whet your dark appetite:

**Black Iris**  Deepest violet in color and with a fluttery shape and velvety texture, these deliciously scented blossoms are the epitome of dark elegance.

**Whipple's Beardtongue**  With goblet-shaped blossoms that seem to be spilling drops of magenta-hued blood, this herb makes a beautiful addition to any bouquet.

**Black Dahlia**  Even if these flowers didn't share their name with a murdered 1940s siren, their lush, black-red color might bring blood to mind.

# Pets and Familiars

veryone enjoys pets, even vampires. However, nightwalkers are particular in their choice of animal companions, preferring to spend their time with exotic creatures.

These human servants hope for the ultimate payoff from their vampire master. Familiars will often carry out errands for vampire covens as a form of apprenticeship, earning their trust and learning appropriate conduct. Most familiars bear a coven tattoo (also known as a glyph) and donate blood to their masters. Successful apprentices are eventually turned into vampires.

A common form for vampires to shapeshift into, bats are often close companions of the vampire race. Naturally, a vampire bat is the most suitable choice, as this creature will share its master's feeding habits and long lifespan.

Though many humans care for spiders as pets, spiders (particularly fearsome giant tarantulas) are particularly well suited to vampires. Easily transported, spiders have minimal needs and are incredibly hardy, helpful for a life of travel. It is for this reason that they are the favored pet of choice for transient vampires.

Partial to a moth-based menu, scorpions are the ideal pet for vampires living in dusty, crumbling conditions. For mortals, scorpions are not the cuddliest of pets, due to their propensity to pinch and sting with dangerous venom; however, this is not a factor for vampires, who are impervious to scorpion venom.

Considered the ultimate symbols of lust and evil, snakes are natural companions for the discerning and seductive vampire. These louche layabouts require warmth and the odd live morsel to keep them happy.

Renfield, the solicitor rendered mad under Dracula's thrall, became obsessed with insects, setting up extensive traps so that he could eat and observe them. His love of bugs was matched only by his love for Dracula. Exotic pet stores may offer giant hissing Madagascar cockroaches, praying mantises, and other strange multilegged beasts.

Like bats, rats are another loyal pet and forever willing to do a vampire's bidding. Nocturnal, intelligent, and easy to train, they feel happiest when surrounded by other rats. Remember: Rats do require a great deal of attention and exercise, so they'll need a loving vampire to tend to their needs.

The father of dogs, a wild forebear to its more timid descendants, the wolf answers to no ordinary owner. Wolves live best in pairs and have detailed needs best tended by a dedicated vampire master upon whom they can imprint unswerving loyalty. (Please note: Werewolves are different from common wolves, are disliked by vampires, and do not make suitable gifts for vampire friends.)

Not every vamp can drive a slick Porsche or a Gothically modified hearse. But you can always vamp your ride—with matte black paint, velvet seat covers, and tinted windows for those sunny days.

A Gothic car at the Burning Man Festival →

# FANGAPALOOZA
## SOUNDS FOR THE SOULLESS

A song haunts the ears, sending the listener drifting into an enthralled reverie. It's only natural that vampires yearn for unnatural music. A well-tuned piece can hypnotize the ears, stir the blood, and agitate the senses.

## A Taste for the Classics

In older times, vampires enjoyed classical pieces and ventured out into the night's chill to visit opera houses and symphonies. Classical music has the ability to create the dramatic emotions vampires so enjoy. Some pieces sweep with melodrama, such as Wagner's *Die Walküre*, or gently meander, such as Liszt's *A Symphony to Dante's Divina Commedia*. But the ultimate would have to be "O Fortuna" from Orff's *Carmina Burana*, which sounds like the very plummet into a hellish eternity.

## A More Bleeding-Edge Discography

Today, most vampires have cultivated more modern and edgy musical tastes, and nightclubs have risen up across the world to cater to them. Though some vamps still harbor affection for the classics, many have embraced the infectiousness of techno and raves or the gothic tones of industrial music and death metal. Some must-haves for your collection are listed at right, but don't let them limit you. Know that there are as many ways to enjoy eternal music as there are to enjoy eternity. If your tastes run to Britpop or Bollywood, who's to say that this music can't also feed your undead soul?

**Angelspit** An Australian band that combines industrial, cyberpunk, and goth sounds.

**Android Lust** Industrial darkwave that skips and blends gothic genres.

**AFI** Rural California's finest blend of emo-melodic hardcore with post-punk raucousness.

**Bauhaus** Considered the first gothic rock group. Singer Peter Murphy's appearance performing "Bela Lugosi's Dead" in *The Hunger* pleased vampire lovers worldwide.

**Cannibal Corpse** Controversial gods of death metal.

**The Cramps** Seminal psychobilly and midnight garage music meet in one package.

**Einstürzende Neubauten** Everlasting avant-garde German industrial troupe.

**My Chemical Romance** Emo rock with a grand sense of ceremony, and great clothes.

**Nine Inch Nails** Seemingly undead industrial outfit led by the indomitable Trent Reznor.

**Puscifer** Moody, atmospheric experiments from Maynard James Keenan.

**Rammstein** Epic industrial hard rock from Germany.

**The Sisters of Mercy** Legendary London goth act known for their brooding and thunderous style.

# Music for All Eternity

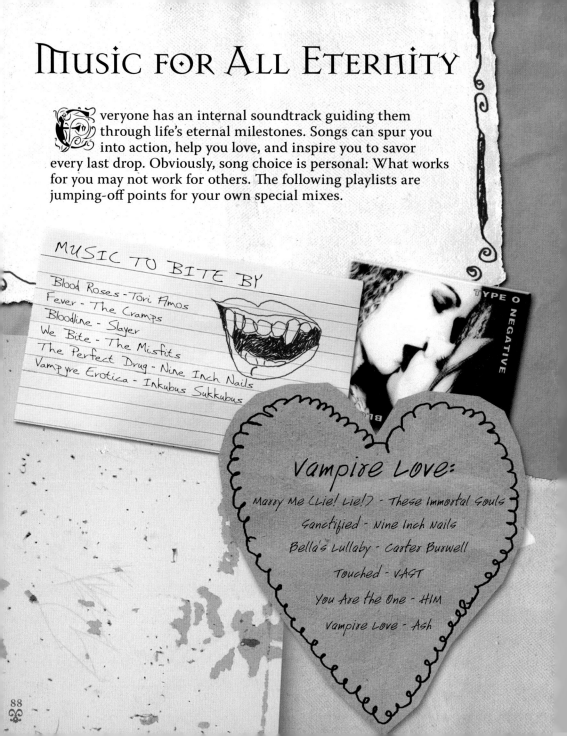

veryone has an internal soundtrack guiding them through life's eternal milestones. Songs can spur you into action, help you love, and inspire you to savor every last drop. Obviously, song choice is personal: What works for you may not work for others. The following playlists are jumping-off points for your own special mixes.

## MUSIC TO BITE BY

Blood Roses - Tori Amos
Fever - The Cramps
Bloodline - Slayer
We Bite - The Misfits
The Perfect Drug - Nine Inch Nails
Vampyre Erotica - Inkubus Sukkubus

## Vampire Love:

Marry Me (Lie! Lie!) - These Immortal Souls

Sanctified - Nine Inch Nails

Bella's Lullaby - Carter Burwell

Touched - VAST

You Are the One - HIM

Vampire Love - Ash

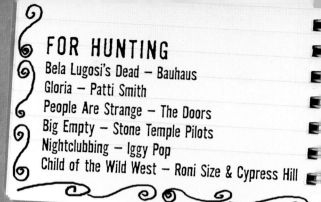

# FOR HUNTING
Bela Lugosi's Dead — Bauhaus
Gloria — Patti Smith
People Are Strange — The Doors
Big Empty — Stone Temple Pilots
Nightclubbing — Iggy Pop
Child of the Wild West — Roni Size & Cypress Hill

## TO PLAY IN THE DARK
Black Celebration — Depeche Mode
Black Sun — Dead Can Dance
Black Flowers — Chris Isaak
Paint It Black — The Rolling Stones
Black Widow — Kyuss

## FOR BEING TURNED

LULLABY - THE CURE

LET ME SIGN - ROBERT PATTINSON

THIS CORROSION - SISTERS OF MERCY

TUPELO - NICK CAVE & THE BAD SEEDS

MORE HUMAN THAN HUMAN - ROB ZOMBIE

BLACK NO. 1 - TYPE O NEGATIVE

## FOR DRESSING UP

HALLOWEEN — MINISTRY

FLAMING RED — ADAM ANT

BAD KIDS — BLACK LIPS

CAPE FEAR — UNIDENTIFIED FLYING ORCHESTRA

BLACK MIRROR — ARCADE FIRE

MAKE-UP — ELEFANT

# Vampire Party
## HAVE THE TIME OF YOUR (NON)LIFE

 ow that you know about the best vampire music, you'll have vampires and vampire-lovers alike clamoring at your door for an invite. Let them in and host a feast for immortals!

## DECK THE CRYPT

Release the bats! Hang rubber bats from corners and around tables to make your vampire-kin feel at home (or crypt). Drape black cloth over curtains, chairs, and mirrors, and fashion coffins from cardboard boxes.

## PLAN A MENU TO DIE FOR

**Steak Tartare** Offer raw steak hash marinated with wine and seasonings, served with an egg yolk, capers, and toast. Vampires partial to raw meat, especially those who can digest, adore this dish. If you make this, use the freshest and best-quality ingredients, lest your food-poisoned vampire guest make you his next meal.

**Blood Shots** Heat up thick, red tomato soup and pour into individual shot glasses. Garnish with a fresh basil leaf and serve hot.

**Bloody Sweet** Bake a red velvet layer cake. Once it's cooled, spread jelly or dyed-red whipped cream on the bottom layer, then sprinkle it with fresh red berries. Place the other half on top and drizzle with a red syrup, preferably a berry coulis.

## DRINK DEEP

**Virgin Bloody Mary** Fill a glass with ice. Pour in 6 ounces (175 ml) tomato juice and 2 tsp each Worcestershire and Tabasco sauce. Shake in salt and pepper. Garnish with a lemon slice and a stick of celery.

**Fangria** Mix one bottle of organic grape juice with 4 ounces (120 ml) each cranberry and orange juices. Add 2 ounces (60 ml) lime juice and 1.5 ounces (45 ml) sugar syrup. Add slices of pear, apple, orange, lemon, and lime in fang-friendly pieces.

**Virgin Sea Breeze** Shake up 0.5 ounces (15 ml) grenadine with 3 ounces (90 ml) each cranberry and white grapefruit juices, then pour into an ice-laden glass. No grenadine? Add superfine sugar to cold pomegranate juice and shake for a few minutes.

## PLAYING A (NOT-SO) DANGEROUS GAME

Spray-paint some rubber bats gold and award "Batties" to the best performers in the following games.

**Inside the Vampires' Studio** Project your favorite vampire film onto a wall, turn down the sound, and get your friends to act out the scenes. Appoint judges to score, and then put on a less-refined version of the Oscars. (Just be sure to cap the acceptance speech lengths: Your winners could truly ramble on and on forever.)

**Fangata** Put glitter into balloons before blowing them up. Blindfold participants and have them try to pop the balloons with a fork or sharpened stake. The winner not only wins a Batty; the burst of glitter will also give him or her a spontaneous *Twilight* makeover.

# SHOULD YOU DATE A MORTAL?

ove is often completely out of a vampire's control. Even vampires don't get to choose whom they love, and often Cupid's bow hits upon a truly unsuitable paramour—like a mortal.

## LOVE AT FIRST BITE

In comparison to vampires, mortals are fragile beings of blood and bone. Their faces flush, they take faltering steps, they age. These frail creatures nevertheless can pose a threat to your immortality. Heartbreak, exposure, and unnecessary risk-taking are all possibilities to contend with if your true love is a mortal human. But if your heart compels you to seek happiness with a mortal soulmate, here are some key concerns to consider.

❋ **Rejection** If they don't know of your vampire status when you start dating, the odds are they soon will. How will they react? Perhaps you'll get lucky and hear "Tell me more" instead of "Get away from me!"

❋ **Exposure** Though vampires are adept at secrecy, some mortals are not so discreet. Intentionally or not, they may disclose your supernatural status to others—an uncomfortable eventuality that may force you to leave your loved one, and possibly even your city or state. So that you don't risk your safety for one of the human race's more fickle members, try and give your relationship ample time before disclosing your supernatural identity. Hey, a little secretiveness will only add to your mysterious charms, intriguing your love object even more and hopefully cementing his or her loyalty.

❋ **Annoying Foibles** True love may know no boundaries, but it sure can test your superacute senses. Humans are a notoriously fidgety species—always shifting about and making noise, whereas you are as quiet and calm as, well, the dead. As beings who either enjoy deathlike sleep or don't nap at all, vampires may also find that a human's sleep habits can be quite noisy. Just pack some earplugs if they happen to snore or sleep-talk.

❋ **Temptation** Sometimes heavy petting can get so heavy that you end up snacking on your sweetie. Can you keep a tight rein on your appetites around your new love? Again, it's good to take it slow to prevent disaster.

❋ **Mortal Danger** A vampire is no stranger to battle, but with a new relationship comes a new vulnerability that enemies are eager to exploit. Your boyfriend or girlfriend could become the pawn in a contest between you and a rabid vampire tracker or the object of a powerful vampire's affections, and someone could get hurt. And that someone is not likely to be you.

Ultimately, no one enters relationships as perfect individuals. Many vampires—as well as humans—hide secrets or are less than perfect, yet just as many still find love and acceptance with someone special. So your new honey might be mortal. Accept it and let the relationship take its course. You just might transform each other.

# PLACES TO VISIT NOW THAT YOU'RE UNDEAD

As a vampire, a new world has opened to you, a world begging to be explored and devoured. And though you could visit all the usual tourist sites, why not put some bite into your travel plans with these infamous vampire venues?

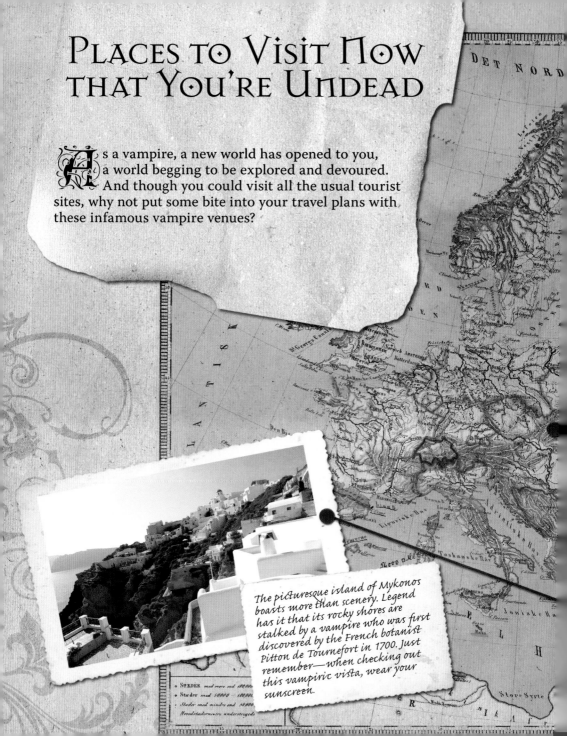

The picturesque island of Mykonos boasts more than scenery. Legend has it that its rocky shores are stalked by a vampire who was first discovered by the French botanist Pitton de Tournefort in 1700. Just remember—when checking out this vampiric vista, wear your sunscreen.

Begin your tour with the infamous Bran Castle in Transylvania, the rumored home of the real-life Dracula— or at least a castle that inspired Bram Stoker for his 1897 novel.

Enjoy a view of Slovakian hills from Čachtice Castle, home to vampire Erzsébet Báthory.

# Travel Hot Spots

### Romania: a Pilgrimage to the Motherland

In addition to Bran Castle, the majestic forests of Transylvania hide two other castles tied to Vlad the Impaler, also known as Dracula: the gothic Hunyad Castle, which served as his prison, and the intimidating Poenari Castle, perched perilously atop a cliff face. Both castles are reputed to be haunted, and Poenari Castle in particular is rumored to be the most haunted place in the world. Listen closely—can you hear the rumblings of the dead?

### New Orleans: Down by the Bayou

Sweaty, sexy, and sinful: New Orleans is like Disneyland for vampires. This humid wonderland has housed many vampires who adore the mixture of high-class and seedy. Filled with stunning period homes and a vibrant music scene, New Orleans has a rich history of supernatural power.

### Forks, Washington: Looking for All that Shimmers

The Pacific Northwest not only hides the sun; it also hides vampires. Let your skin cool in the misty rains while you enjoy the beaches, forests, and small-town charm. Look out for groups of impossibly good-looking and aloof people: What is their secret?

### Mexico: on the Trail of the Chupacabra

Grab your cryptozoology hat and track down the mysterious goatsucker. Though notoriously shy, it can be found. Look for local reports of unexplained livestock deaths for clues. Time your trip for November 2nd, the Day of the Dead—the one day it's considered normal to be the walking dead.

### London: Dracula Dreaming

Recreate the Victorian drama of Dracula's London tour. This metropolis crumbles with gothic gloom and grandeur. Cut a swath through Covent Garden's maze and run around the labyrinth of streets at night to feel the heat of the chase. Visit West Norwood Cemetery and see what's stirring.

### Greek Isles: the Rare Sun-and-Sand Vamp

The Mediterranean islands of Mykonos and Crete are legendary breeding grounds for the *vrykolakas*, a Greek vampire that can walk by day and causes nightmares. The revenant bodies of those who died after lives of great sin (or, oddly enough, who were born on Christmas or other holy days), the *vrykolakas* must be disinterred and burned to ashes.

### Slovakia: the Bloody Countess

Rumored to bathe in the blood of her female servants, the Countess Erzsébet Báthory is known as the most vicious serial killer in history and is often referred to as the female Dracula. The countess—who is to this day believed to have been a vampire—was placed under house arrest at Čachtice Castle while European nobility uncovered her atrocities, which included the sacrifice of several noble daughters. Today, the castle lies in ruins within a national nature reserve.

# THIRTY WAYS TO FILL
# ETERNITY

## 1 ROCKET OFF: IN SPACE NO ONE CAN HEAR YOU FEED

You're ageless, so why not be weightless? Book a seat as a space tourist and travel upward. Take a familiar to keep up your blood stocks and escape detection. The perpetual night will keep you at ease, and you'll have a view that is out of this world.

## 2 DIVE THROUGH THE STARRY SKIES

Test your mettle and jump out into the night sky. Although many like to sky-dive during the day to see the world below, night diving is recommended for sun-sensitive vampires. (Plus, you can review your escape routes from above.)

## 3 CALL ON THE MINIONS

Need an army? Bats are the answer. Stand in awe as a bat colony ascends under a setting sun, darkening the dusk with their wings. Some great bat-spotting places include Bracken Cave, Texas (a 20 million–strong bat colony), or Melbourne, Australia, where colonies depart the Botanic Gardens just as movies and plays are starting, for added drama.

## 4 STAND UNDER THE AURORA BOREALIS

Long feared by Inuits and Laplanders, the flickering flames that light wintry night skies were once thought to be vengeful gods and ghosts. Stand under the flares for an unmatchable surge of power.

## 5 GO ON: BE NICE TO A WEREWOLF JUST ONCE

Listen, we know there's a feud going on and no one wants to talk to one another, but this is just silly. Broaden your horizons: Buy a werewolf a cup of coffee and talk with him. Odds are you have an enemy in common—and aren't all friendships, at the heart of it, based on inter-supernatural-species blood feuds, anyway?

## 6 PAY YOUR RESPECTS IN VENICE

Long considered a city of old-world charm and mystery, Venice is also the final resting place of the exhumed body of a vampire from the sixteenth century who was found with a rock wedged into her mouth. Make a humble visit to the crypt of this early martyr, and get lost in a labyrinth of sumptuous intrigue.

## 7 INVEST IN THE STOCK MARKET

An eternal life requires eternal wealth. Savvy vamps set up numerous investment accounts to fund their lifestyle. In a pinch, they can help you set up a new persona when you need it.

## 8 SET UP MULTIPLE RESIDENCES

Investing in real estate is always a great idea, and more than one home is even better. Tour your different homes for a change of pace, to escape unwanted attention, or just to enjoy different seasons and tastes. Stayed in one home too long? Take off for a few generations to avoid suspicion.

## 9 AVOID THE SUN ON SEVEN DIFFERENT CONTINENTS

Travel the world and set your shadowed foot on every landmass. Hitch a ride on a cargo boat and see the world at your leisure. Be sure to drink in the sights, sounds, and civilians that you encounter—travel will make you a citizen of the world, transforming you in unexpected ways.

## 10 MEET THE WORLD-CHANGERS

With supernatural charm and persuasion on your side, you can talk your way around anything. Why not into anything? As an immortal you have the chance to meet the people who truly change the world for the better. Finagle your way into the inner circles to meet presidents, scientists, artists, and other revolutionary pioneers.

## 11 BE SOMEONE'S HERO

Not everyone is as strong as a vampire. Don't be afraid to step in and protect someone who needs your assistance. Then nonchalantly brush it off and deny helping at all.

## 12 Face Your Fears

Spend a night in a haunted house or castle where others fear to tread. Stand, er, fang to phantasm and show them you're unmiffed. Not afraid of ghosts? Try facing something else that terrifies your immortal soul. Once you've faced fear, you can face anything. (Except the sun. And wooden stakes. And perhaps garlic.)

## 13 Save a Wolf

Wolves have long been stalwart companions to vampires, but many are on the endangered list. Why not spend time helping out a wolf conservation group, looking after wolves or replanting their habitat? If the wolf isn't your type of creature, find another species to help.

## 14 Jump on the Scariest Roller Coaster

Jump onto the scariest roller coaster you can find, and see who can inspire true terror: you or the ride.

## 15 Flirt with Something Living

Plant a tree somewhere and visit regularly to tend to its needs. Once it gets to a reasonable size, carve your initials into the trunk. As it grows, you will continue to defy time. See who lasts longer.

## 16 Create Multiple Identities

With slayers and bounty hunters constantly looking for known vampires, it's worthwhile to develop a slew of fake identities. A series of identities—all with their own properties, passports, licenses, and blood-bank memberships—will help you feel like a new person no matter what the situation.

## 17 Capture Your Beauty

Supreme loveliness such as yours should be memorialized in a portrait. How else can you appreciate your dazzling looks, if you're one of the many vampires cruelly prevented from seeing yourself in a mirror? And even if your looks are immune to the unjustices of passing time, everyone wants a good profile pic these days.

## 18 Get a Secret-Keeper and Tell Them Your Life Story, No Holds Barred

Often cool and aloof, vampires are possibly the most secretive people in the world. Find a worthy ally or biographer to keep your secrets and record your history. Strangely, vampire researchers are often best for this duty, as they are so fascinated with the species. Who knows? Your story may even become a best seller!

## 19 Find the Abominable Snowman or Sasquatch and Beat It in a Bare-Knuckle Brawl

What's the point of all your superior hunting and fighting skills if you can't take on these feared and mysterious mountain mammals? Track them down and challenge them to a fight. There's no need to fight fatally: Just let them know who's standing at the top of the cryptozoological food chain.

## 20 Hop on the Orient Express

For the discerning traveler with specific needs, this iconic long-distance passenger train will take you from England to Eastern Europe in style. Note: You will be required to bring lunch.

## 21 Begin a Collection

Ever wonder how people amass amazing art, antiques, or comic books? Keep an eye out for first-edition books, designers who craft furniture by hand, or art that compels a quickening of your dead heart. With eternity on your side, you'll have a world-class collection in no time.

## 22 Get Reading

Dumb vampires don't survive. Hole up in a nearby crypt or crumbling mansion and read every great work of fiction you can find. Devour encyclopedias and dictionaries with relish. Expand your mind and your life span in the process.

## 23 Try Something Different on the Menu

Oh yes, we're going there. Consider broadening your palate by branching out from traditional meals of human blood: venison, rabbit, or, that lobster of the land, the armadillo. Any new taste will send your enhanced senses overboard: It could be just the change you're looking for.

## 24 Recapture the Night

No one knows the sights you've seen—unless you're taking photos. Consider taking up night photography to create a journal dedicated to the night. Only you know the night's rich shadows and colors. Share your view with others.

## 25 Take on a Protégé

Newborn vampires can be foundlings, without a sire to guide them through eternity. Why not find a like-minded deathly debutante and introduce them to the fangier things in life? They'll learn, and you'll gain a lifelong friend.

## 26 Become a Hollywood Agent

A perfect career choice for any self-respecting vamp: all the glamour, riches, and power, but none of that pesky media attention or day shoots. Those poor actors have no idea what awaits them on the casting couch.

## 27 See Halley's Comet

One of the benefits of being immortal is that centennial events are easy to wait for. Why not keep a calendar of comets and greet each one like an old friend? Halley's comet returns every seventy-five years. Look out for the Encke, Wolf, and Swift-Tuttle comets in the skies to show your mastery of time. But remember: It only counts when you see it a second time.

## 28 Fall in Love

Love is the ultimate in transformation. No one should walk through eternity alone, at least not all of the time. Find someone who accepts and cherishes the best parts of you and challenges you to become even better.

## 29 Start a Family—a Coven Family

Although you cannot have cute little demon babies of your own (let's just say the universe believes in safe sex for vampires), you can still build a family. Reach out to fellow vampires who feel like family and start your own coven.

## 30 Live Forever

Think of this as the list item that you will never need to cross off. Gifted with immortality, you will outlive every living thing. Well, you will if you remember to act wisely.

# ARMCHAIR
# VAMPIRE

## A MOST HALLOWED TOUR OF VAMPIRE HISTORY AND CULTURE

**B**ewitching humans with whispered stories, your undead kin have long enticed their victims with the most compelling bait of all: fascination. Now that you have joined the ranks of the immortal, it is time to study the many gifts your vampire brethren have granted society.

For the cultured elite, we will linger over the immortals' contributions to culture over time. Learn how vampires have performed through the ages—as grotesque and glorious muses that have inspired poets, writers, artists, and filmmakers—to commemorate their terrifying appetites.

For those of you with a more archaeological interest, we will wend our way through the annals of history to uncover testimony and physical evidence proving the existence of vampires.

Knowledge is power, gentle reader. Just how powerful do you wish to become? Settle into your chaise longue and read as the vampire's historical roots and depictions in the arts unfurl before you.

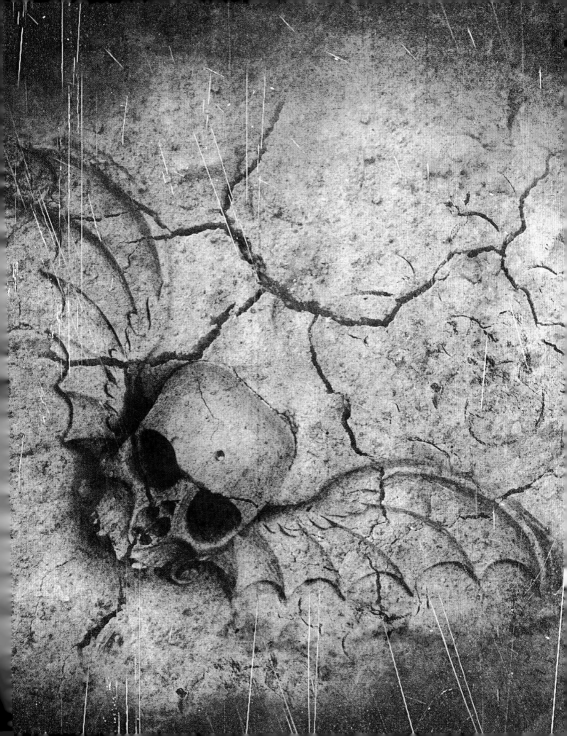

# HOW DEEP IS YOUR UNDEAD KNOWLEDGE?

 n the shadowed school of the occult, do you stand at the head of the class, or do you wear the dunce's cap? This quiz will reveal your standing, and guide you to suitable tutors of the darkness.

### NAME A COMIC BOOK VAMPIRE.

A. Blade.
B. Death.
C. The Immortal Kevin.

### ACCORDING TO LEGEND, A VAMPIRE SLEEPS BEST WHEN SURROUNDED BY

A. His or her native soil.
B. Black velvet drapes.
C. Sentries standing guard against the sunlight.

### THE *BAOBHAN SITH* CANNOT DANCE OR DRAIN A PERSON PROTECTED BY

A. Spears fashioned from yew.
B. Magical garments.
C. Iron objects, including horseshoes.

### RAYNE IS A MEMBER OF

A. The Pussycat Dolls.
B. Parliament.
C. The Brimstone Society.

### INTO EVERY GENERATION IS BORN A

A. Slayer.
B. Metallurgist.
C. Witch.

### THE *D* IN VAMPIRE HUNTER D STANDS FOR

A. *Dramamine.* Vampires get seasick.
B. *Dracula,* also his father's name.
C. *Djibouti.*

### THE VOLTURI ARE A COLLECTION OF

A. Gifted and feared vampire rulers from Italy.
B. Shapely women bringing about a fashion revolution.
C. Vampire assassins.

### A CANADIAN VAMPIRE POLICEMAN WAS FEATURED ON WHAT SHOW?

A. *Truc Blood.*
B. *Angel.*
C. *Forever Knight.*

### A FAMOUS TALE OF VAMPIRES OVERRUNNING A SMALL TOWN TAKES PLACE IN

A. Mount Waverley.
B. Salem's Lot.
C. Berry, Maine.

## Bella Swan Falls in Love with

A. Edward Cullen.
B. Eric Vlad.
C. Spike.

## The Traditional Dracula Is Based on

A. Vlad the Sommelier.
B. Vlad Tepes, aka Vlad the Impaler of the Dracul.
C. Bram Stoker's real-life experiences as a slayer.

## Selene, a Beautiful and Deadly Vampire, Belongs to

A. The Watchers' Council.
B. Team Fang, a bloodthirsty cabal.
C. The Death Dealers, a crack team of vampire warriors.

## Lamia Was Half-Human, Half . . .

A. Wild boar.
B. Tulip.
C. Slithering snake.

## What Do Werewolves and Vampires Think of One Another?

A. They are total BFFs, holding slumber parties and braiding each other's hair.
B. They are sworn enemies at worst, and hold uneasy truces at best.
C. They couldn't care less about each other—who could be bothered with a bunch of ill-behaved dogs/filthy bloodsuckers?

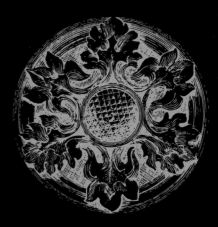

## Answers (Score 2 points for every correct question):

1. A  2. A  3. C  4. C  5. A  6. B
7. A  8. C  9. B  10. A  11. B  12. C
13. C  14. B

**0–8** You realize this is a book about vampires, right? Do you even know what vampires are? Reread this book and open your mind to the darkness before embarking upon the heavy scholarship contained in this chapter. You have a lot of studying ahead of you.

**8–18** You're not the sharpest fang around, but this chapter contains many facts on which you can sharpen your wits (and canines). Immerse yourself in the vampire lore and contributions to the arts presented in the following pages.

**18–28** We bow down to you, anointed one. Long has your arrival been prophesized. Do as destiny demands: Take your place as Vampire Master.

# THE HISTORICAL EVIDENCE OF VAMPIRES

**W**hile mortals may foolishly ignore evidence of the supernatural realm and scoff at noble vampire traditions, the undead have left some tantalizing footprints throughout history: the person who escaped with a terrifying tale, the body that did not crumple into dust, or the vampire hunter who left a record of his work.

## VAMPIRE TOOLS

Packed into small briefcases made of leather and wood, vampire-hunting kits have long been indispensable to slayers. These cases were lined and outfitted with knives, wooden stakes, bibles, rosary beads, and vials. Interested in buying one? You can find an odd gem via online auctions or antique dealers. Kits bearing the name of Professor Blomberg or Nicholas Plomdeur are re-creations, though still delightful relics.

## THE WRITTEN WORD

Historians have recorded sightings of vampires for centuries. The earliest record dates to the twelfth century in Walter Map's *De nugis curialium* (*Courtiers' Trifles*), which chronicles the events of his travels. The fearedtome *Malleus Maleficarum* (*The Hammer of Witches*), a great tool of inquisitors, also covered vampires.

## VAMPIRE OUTBREAKS

Though they are rare, some documented cases of vampire campaigns are on record. One of the earlier and most notorious cases occurred around 1250 AD: Eyewitnesses in Moravia (a region of the Czech Republic) recounted seeing a vampire arise at night, rip off his burial shroud, and run naked through the town to feed on slumbering women and children. In another case of reported vampirism, the British historian William of Newburgh (who studied many "revenants" in twelfth-century England) recorded the tale of a man who fell to his death while witnessing his wife's infidelity. After his burial, he arose each night to harass the village around Alnwick Castle, and a mysterious and unidentified epidemic claimed the lives of many villagers. When the man's body was dug up from his grave, it was reportedly full of blood and not at all decomposed. As a general vamp-evasion tactic, people have long dug up suspected vampires and burned their hearts or staked them in place if any blood was found in them. There are many artifacts and sites in existence that testify to this gruesome though effective trend.

## THE VENETIAN VAMP

A recent excavation in Venice unearthed something quite unearthly: a sixteenth-century vampire burial. Interred among plague-ridden corpses on the island of Lazzaretto Nuovo, the woman had a brick wedged into her mouth to stop her from chewing through her shroud and rising.

# FAMOUS
# REAL-LIFE VAMPIRES

These reputed vampires have stalked throughout history, their tales the stuff of wonder and terror. Many writers have looked to them for inspiration. But who were they? Are the tales told about them true, or are they just the panicky propaganda of a horrified populace? One thing is sure: Their bloodlusts were fierce and deadly.

## VLAD TEPES (1431–1476)

The prince of Wallachia and heir of the Dracul, Vlad the Impaler had a definitive leadership style. While some of the horror ascribed to him can be considered rumor, some facts are known. His unquenchable thirst for terror is shown through such infamous acts as nailing hats to men's heads and his gruesome love of impaling his adversaries. One of the most famous woodcuts of this ruler shows him dining within a forest of impaled victims. The legend of Vlad is the basis of the vampire that we know and fear today, as he inspired Bram Stoker's *Dracula*.

## ERZSÉBET BÁTHORY (1560–1614)

This vain aristocrat, also known as the Blood Countess of Hungary, supposedly bathed in the blood of her victims—who numbered as many as 650. An accomplished leader who protected the populace from advancing forces, she became infamous for luring young girls with the promise of well-paid jobs or etiquette training before imprisoning and killing them. Báthory was tried before the courts and bricked into her castle, dying four years later.

## GILLES DE RAIS (1404–1440)

Known as the inspiration for Bluebeard, this feared warrior didn't confine his bloodshed to the battlefield. Discovered to have possibly killed between 80 and 200 children, this Frenchman cut a swath through France. Once a companion-in-arms to Joan of Arc, the formerly pious Catholic degenerated into a life of unspeakable cruelty and sadism, feasting on the blood and organs of his victims. Debate still rages as to whether his appetites were simply the result of madness or if his evil nature was occult inspired.

## PETER PLOGOJOWITZ (????–1725)

This eighteenth-century Serbian peasant is thought to have gone on a feeding frenzy for eight days after his death. In all, nine villagers died quickly and mysteriously, and all gasped upon their deathbed that it was the work of Plogojowitz. The well-documented hysteria prompted an exhumation with distressing results: The dead body was still growing and filled with blood. Even more telling, his mouth was smeared with blood. His remains were staked and burned.

# Written in Blood
## Vampires in Literature

The world of literature abounds with classic titles that have kept the vampiric world alive. Chronicling demonic successes and excesses, these must-reads will school you in the life immortal. Vampires who have surpassed the concerns of the flesh may find some racy scenes tedious and the content overly focused on mortals and their sad little urges, but still, these are volumes worth consultation.

### "The Vampyre" (1819)
### John Polidori

A tale of tragedy, rebirth, and madness wrought by the bloodsucking Lord Ruthven (based on "mad, bad, and dangerous to know" Lord Byron). Written during the same week and at the same villa as Mary Shelley's *Frankenstein,* Polidori's story deftly gathers all the loose vampire beliefs into a taut thread.

### "Carmilla" (1872)
### Joseph Sheridan Le Fanu

A gloriously gothic story about Carmilla, a mysterious and beautiful vampire who preys upon young women. One of the first vampire novels, it covers shapeshifting and offers handy tips on walking through locked doors.

### *Dracula* (1897)
### Bram Stoker

The unholy bible for those new to the world of vampires. This classic introduces Count Dracula as he plans and executes a very bloody London holiday. An invaluable guide for vampires planning the logistics of long-distance travel and evasion tactics against irrepressible foes.

### *Salem's Lot* (1975)
### Stephen King

A widowed author returns to discover that vampires have overrun his sleepy Maine hometown, turning the populace into bloodsuckers. *Salem's Lot* not only brought vampire literature to a mainstream audience; it also gives priceless advice on how to battle meddling priests.

### The Vampire Chronicles (1976–2003) Anne Rice

This sumptuous, century-sprawling, and prolific series is by the grandmother of gothic, Anne Rice. An indispensable guide to vampire psychology, abilities, and hierarchy for any self-respecting exquisite creature of the night.

### *The Bloody Chamber* (1979)
### Angela Carter

A scathing feminist take on traditional fairy tales, these short stories are not for the faint of heart. Setting ancient tales in more modern times, these hypnotic stories show vampires as creatures rendered desperate by their appetite and need for compassion. Perfect for any empowered female vampire.

### THE GILDA STORIES (1991)
### JEWELLE GOMEZ

*The Gilda Stories* gives the lowdown on sustainable vampirism while gently weaving in African-American history. A slave girl (who later becomes Gilda) recounts her life and travels, offering a realistic account of a vampire's daily life. A kinder and gentler take on traditional vampire narrative with science-fiction overtones.

### LOST SOULS (1992)
### POPPY Z. BRITE

A boy named Nothing, who's always thought there was something different about him, discovers his vampire heritage and faces a terrible choice. There are no high-minded Cullens in *Lost Souls:* The lifestyle championed by these vampires is light on morals and high on sweat-stained sin. Perfect for existentialist and nihilistic vampires wanting to forge their own identity.

### ANITA BLAKE, VAMPIRE HUNTER (1993–2009)
### LAURELL K. HAMILTON

Anita is a strong and resourceful animator and vampire hunter with the Regional Preternatural Investigation Team. Hard-boiled detective stories with a cast of zombies, shapeshifters, vampires, and fairies make this the all-purpose series for anyone new to the supernatural world.

### BLOODSUCKING FIENDS (1995)
### CHRISTOPHER MOORE

This fun and fast-paced vampire tale is about modern life, love, and getting used to being a vampire in San Francisco. A sequel, *You Suck: A Love Story*, features diary excerpts from goth teen Abby Normal, making it the real guide for modern-day vampires (and those who love them).

### THE SOUTHERN VAMPIRE MYSTERIES (2001–2009)
### CHARLAINE HARRIS

The basis for the popular TV series *True Blood,* Harris's books focus on the emerging vampire community in small-town Louisiana and offer invaluable tips for vampires wanting to live openly with humans. Seen through the eyes of the telepathic Sookie Stackhouse, who is thrown into the deep end of intrigue, blood, and romance.

### TWILIGHT (2005–2008)
### STEPHENIE MEYER

This staggeringly popular series tells the story of teenage love between teen Bella Swan and 104-year-old Edward Cullen in the perpetually misty town of Forks, Washington. Invaluable guide for those dating brooding vegetarian vampires.

### VAMPIRE ACADEMY (2007–2010) RICHELLE MEAD

Two vampire teens face the most dangerous threat of all: school. Juggling their strengths and vulnerabilities, the teen girls navigate a treacherous path among *dhampirs* and both *moroi* and *strigoi* vampires.

### THE STRAIN (2009)
### GUILLERMO DEL TORO AND CHUCK HOGAN

The award-winning director and author team up with this modern-day vampire thriller. Set in New York City, this book offers a blueprint for vampires wishing to take over the world.

# THE SILVER SCREAM

ince the early days, filmmakers have been under the thrall of vampires—for good reason. Strong, beautiful, and famous for their taboo appetites, vampires are irresistible. Films have kept vampire lore alive, placing them in new worlds and new situations with new powers and threats. What can you, the recently minted or aspiring child of the night, learn from this most morbid of film studies? Observe the ways of the masters in their various habitats, from crumbling European castles and historic New Orleans to suburban wastelands and deepest Africa. A mere mortal could do worse than drink it all in.

## STRIKE TERROR INTO HEARTS—SILENTLY

In *Nosferatu* (1922), the first film ever to depict vampires, the terrifyingly demonic Count Orlok isn't handsome or charming (like today's vampires), but his menacing aura is impressive indeed. The silent film created an ethereal veil of terror that has not been lifted since.

## SINK YOUR FANGS IN OLD-SCHOOL–STYLE

The Count you've come to count on was introduced in 1931's *Dracula*. Suave, hypnotic, and urbane—a flick of his cape and the femmes fall under his thrall. This role made Bela Lugosi famous; it also became the basis for all classic vamps.

## ONE CAN CHEW ON NECKS AS WELL AS SCENERY

Want to achieve the classical vamp stance with a touch of ham? *The Horror of Dracula* (1958) comes from Hammer Films, a university for kitschy monsters. Learn how to strike fear into the heaving chests of doe-eyed ladies and rule over your army of madly flapping rubber bats.

## YOU CAN RULE THE WORLD

Oh yes, dreams can come true. In a time when vampires rule the land, only one human remains: *The Last Man on Earth* (1964). With spooky music, double exposures, and a station wagon slayermobile, this film is perfect for vapid vamp film nights. Based on Richard Matheson's novel, it has been adapted twice more with Charlton Heston (*The Omega Man*) and Will Smith (*I Am Legend*).

## KEEP SOME SOUL

If you're the type of vampire who wants to keep it real with a soulful '70s vibe, *Blacula* (1972) gives the inside word on badass equal-opportunity neck macking and princess hunting. No one is safe in this blaxploitation cult classic—not even clichéd interior designers with really big Afros.

## GLAM AND EURO FOR ETERNITY

*The Hunger* (1983), featuring Catherine Deneuve, David Bowie, and a performance by Bauhaus over the opening credits, is a must-see for aspiring vampires who crave an elegant, modern goth style.

# For Further Vampire Viewing

## Love Thy Neighbor

Discover the pitfalls of living next door to mortals (especially nosy teenagers) in *Fright Night* (1985). The comedy features uniquely gruesome makeup and performances by Roddy McDowall and Chris Sarandon. Definitely a film-at-midnight option for those who prefer giggles over horror.

## Bad, Bad Boys

For the rebel at heart (whether that heart is beating or not), *The Lost Boys* (1987) is a textbook lesson on casual teen-vampire cool. Also to be studied for cautionary information on modern vampire hunters, pitfalls to avoid, and truly unfortunate haircuts.

## True Love Never Dies

It's the new benchmark of love: tracking through reincarnations to find your loved one. Gary Oldman's 1992 performance gives humanity and tragedy to the lovestruck *Dracula* never before seen. Style mavens will adore the lush, Klimt-like aesthetic while Dracula courts his lost love.

## Consider Your True Nature

Does your bloodlust make you a special creature with immortal powers or just an addict? Abel Ferrara's film *The Addiction* (1995) investigates this dilemma through the eyes of Kathleen, a young philosophy student in the process of turning. *The Addiction* is a challenging film for vampires who are in the midst of reevaluating their diets and hunting styles.

## Get Food Delivered Straight to Your Crypt

*From Dusk Till Dawn* (1996) shows how a coven of vampires can set up a small business to bring in both money and food. It's comically visceral in every way and an assault on the senses. Salma Hayek steals the film with her arousing performance.

## Develop an Interest in Antiques

In John Carpenter's *Vampires* (1998), the vicious vamp Valek is closing in on a rare antiquity: the Black Cross of Berziers. It was used on Valek in an incomplete exorcism ritual, and he has since hunted it to vanquish his main vulnerability: sunlight.

## Get Ready for Your Close-up

Have a hankering for a cinematic career? *Shadow of the Vampire* (2000) is a (questionably) fictional account of the filming of vamp classic *Nosferatu*. The crew suspects that their lead actor isn't just playing a vampire—he is a vampire. Stellar performances turn this film into a sobering ode to obsession and loneliness.

## Get in the Heat of the Battle

If you're the type who enjoys working out your issues on the battlefield, you should consider a feud with Lycans (aka werewolves). In *Underworld* (2003), Selene works as a Death Dealer who hunts them, seeking revenge for their role in the death of her family.

## Party Like It's 30 Days of Perpetual Night!

Hankering for a holiday to relax and dine at your leisure? In the smart Swedish flick *Frostbitten* (2006), a mother and daughter try to prevent vampires from wreaking havoc. Effortlessly blending horror and comedy with a smart story, *Frostbitten* is definitely one to watch in the daylight if you're mortal.

## Show Commitment to Your Job

Looking for work? Why not join the Day Watch team, who monitors the do-gooders? In *Night Watch* (2004) and *Day Watch* (2006), vamps are just one of many otherworldly people in a struggle between good and evil. Set in Moscow, the films suck you into a different reality with their frenetic pace and dazzling special effects.

## Young Love Is Forever

Aspiring members of the vampire clan uncertain whether a loved one can give the eternal kiss would do well to study *Twilight* (2008), an educational tale of beauty and yearning. Is your boyfriend a vampire? If you're lucky, he'll not only be a vampire— he'll be another Edward Cullen.

## How to Win Friends and Influence People

Unsure how to make friends? *Let The Right One In* (2008) shows how you, too, can make pals with those around you, even humans. Oskar, a bullied twelve-year-old, notices that something is different about his new neighbor, Eli. Strangely, horror and sweetness combine in a stunning and starkly terrifying way.

Throughout history, vampires have fascinated mortals. Books, films, plays, and songs have been dedicated to their fatal beauty, as mortals foolishly attempt to understand the unknowable.

Theater scene from *Interview with the Vampire* (1994) →

# Small Screen, Big Dreams

Television can't quit with the vampified lovin'. Since the '60s, more and more vampire shows and characters have filled the airways. During this time, the vampires have evolved from staid to stylish, scary, sexy, satanic, and sarcastic. For vamps who have grown up with these characters (or study them in their later afterlife), they can seem like one big high-school class filled with princesses, dreamboats, bullies, and beloved older teachers. Plus, of course, a few bad apples.

## DARK SHADOWS

Long-running gothic soap opera in the 1960s and '70s featured werewolves, ghosts, zombies, man-made monsters, witches, warlocks, time travel (into both the past and the future), and a parallel universe. This campy show still has massive cult appeal (it was one of Johnny Depp's childhood faves).

## BUFFY THE VAMPIRE SLAYER

The ultimate vampire show that single-handedly revived the genre and made it über-smart, snarky, and sincere in the process. Buffy Summers is the perpetually burdened vampire slayer tasked with fighting back the Hellmouth. Aided by her talented friends and trusted Watcher, Buffy fights back a slew of wise-cracking vampires, demons, nemeses, and apocalypses. In the follow-up show, *Angel,* the show's most soulful vamp moves to Los Angeles and becomes a supernatural crime fighter. Of course.

## MOONLIGHT

After being sired by his wife on their wedding night, Mick St. John is a vampire private investigator trying to make a difference. He tackles mysteries and sexual tension with the help of reporter Beth Turner. With so many vampires in television spending their eternities to overcome their impulses, it's a wonder people have ever feared bloodsuckers.

## BEING HUMAN

Who said werewolves and vampires hate each other? A vampire, werewolf, and fledgling ghost share friendships and the same house in Bristol, England, as they struggle to get used to daily life and their powers. There are no designer clothes or fancy homes, just real people trying their best in strange situations.

## COUNT DUCKULA

This animated British series focuses on the world's first and only vegetarian vampire duck, a famous entertainer who travels the world to escape the vampire hunter Dr. Von Goosewing. An ancient vampire, Count Duckula lost his blood-guzzling ways when ketchup was used to bring him back to life in a ritual that calls for blood.

## TRUE BLOOD

A very dark and sexy adaptation of the Sookie Stackhouse mysteries, which use vampires' assimilation into society as a metaphor for the civil rights movement. Sookie, a telepath from Bon Temps, Louisiana, is immersed into a world where vampires have their own synthetic food.

# GRAPHIC TALES

The visual glamour of the vamp world lends itself well to the graphic-novel medium. Read up on your colorful kin in the ink-and-blood–drenched pages of graphic novels and manga.

## BITE CLUB

Featuring stunning artwork, this daring series depicts vampires living in the city of Miami who go through mortal drama, such as racial profiling and struggling to legitimize their family businesses. With *Godfather*-style intrigue, racy women, and hard-boiled crime, *Bite Club* is a vamp classic.

## VAMPIRE HUNTER D

*D* is for *dhampir*, the half-human–half-vampire offspring of a post-nuclear world. *D* is also for *Dracula*, this warrior's true name and his famous father. Vampire Hunter D battles vampires and other adversaries despite being shunned by society. A prolific series of graphic novels, the title has spawned manga, video games, and films.

## BUFFY THE VAMPIRE SLAYER

Can't get enough of the Scooby Gang? Though Buffy comics have existed alongside the TV series, once the show ended, the comics became a reader-approved continuation of the story. The comic series is written by the show's creator and producers, and follows the new Slayer Headquarters. Those who still miss Angel should check out *Angel: After the Fall*.

## 30 DAYS OF NIGHT

With stunning, visceral artwork, this comic series covers the unholy vampire feeding frenzy during the prolonged darkness of Alaskan winter. Though the vampires can feed free from sunlight thanks to the long hours of darkness, the cold dampens their hunting skills—allowing a band of surviving mortals to hide and fight back.

## BLADE

The original Daywalker was born on the glossy pages of Marvel comics back in 1973. This comic series is notable for bringing together vampires and vampire hunters from literature, such as the Harker and Van Helsing families and comic luminaries Spider-Man and Ghost Rider.

## HELLSING

Join the fight against the ancient evil that threatens England and the Protestant Church! The Holy Order of Protestant Knights is run by descendants of Abraham Van Helsing, the ultimate vampire hunter and man who forced Alucard (*Dracula* backward) into servitude. A long-running manga title, *Hellsing* has also crossed over to TV.

## BLOODTHIRST

Finally, vampires find their true calling: covert antiterrorism. The Alpha title tracks a vampire heroine as she hunts down a mysterious physicist hell-bent on nuclear destruction. With old-school comic art, secret cabals, and apocalyptic plans aplenty, *Bloodthirst* is a slightly campy but thoroughly fun read.

# THE DEADLIEST GAME

What better way to try on the vampire mind-set than with role-playing games (RPGs) and other amusements? The role-playing experience can grant you some amazing abilities and transport you to intriguing dark worlds. Take on vampire hunters and werewolves, or assume the persona of a vampire hunter to better know your enemy.

## BLOODRAYNE

A female *dhampir* equipped with considerable strength and switchblade arms, Rayne investigates and eradicates vampires for the top-secret Brimstone Society, all while seeking to fulfill a vendetta against her long-lost vampire father. As Rayne, you must hunt and destroy vampires and the nefarious Gegengheist Gruppe (GGG). Compelling story arcs and thrilling action have made this a popular video game.

## VAMPIRE MOONGLOW

Delve into the sleepy town of Forks, Washington, in this role-playing game, where you can assume a personality in the *Twilight* universe. Will you be a mortal, werewolf, or vampire? Will you choose the path of pained enlightenment or carnal appetite, or will you investigate the town's secret? This forum game is an imaginative and collaborative addiction, and possibly the only vampire game where you can fall in love with a fellow player. Who knows whom you will meet?

## VAMPIRE HUNTER D

Get your sword ready to fight more vampires in this adventure and survival game. Charge around a castle in the role of D, battling the Nobles and Barbarois mutants, among other enemies. This Sony PlayStation game,

based on the *Vampire Hunter D: Bloodlust* anime series, can end several ways, depending on your fighting abilities.

## VAMPIRE RAIN

A strain of vampires known as the Nightwalkers are behind a string of disappearances around the world. As a newly minted vampire hunter and member of a covert operations team, you are dropped into a rainy Los Angeles to do battle. Your lack of experience means you have only one factor on your side: Vampire senses are dulled by the rain. A stealth game for Microsoft Xbox and Sony PlayStation 3, it puts a huge arsenal of weapons at your disposal.

## DARKSTALKERS

A cult favorite, especially in Asian arcades, *Darkstalkers* lets you assume a multitude of characters to fight off attacking vampires (aka Darkstalkers). Similar to the classic *Street Fighter,* it is a simple fight game in which you develop signature moves.

## REIGN OF BLOOD

Do you dare answer destiny's call? An online RPG, *Reign of Blood* takes you through Dead City—home to vampires. Attack others (or be attacked!), form allegiances, join covens, cast spells, and rise up the ranks to become all-powerful.

# A FINAL WORD FROM YOUR GRATEFUL AUTHOR

## WHEREIN THE UNGENTLE READER IS BID FAREWELL INTO THE DARK COVENANT OF ETERNITY

The chill of the Dark Embrace has been bestowed upon you, and immortality now lies at your feet. You are at one with the shadows. You are vampire.

Where will the night take you? Will you follow the legends of base appetite and fright, or may you assent to a life of pure, exquisite refinement? All has been explained—all you need do now is explore.

You have received aesthetic advice pertaining to dress, artwork, and interiors and been counseled on the appropriate history, legends, and physiology of our species, cataloging the many different kinds of vampires.

You have explored your burgeoning powers with detailed instructions on development. From here, you can show yourself as a knowledgeable and cultivated creature of the night, one bestowed with confidence and awareness.

True awareness comes from understanding all of your gifts—your superior physical abilities, your cognitive blessings, and how your kind have acted as muses to cultures across the world, appearing in the arts and lurking in that most feared human alcove: the subconscious.

After such tutelage, all that remains is your participation. Upon which path will you tread? Where will you go, dear fledgling child of the night? What will you do and how will you be?

Herewith, you have shared in this humble store of knowledge. Now it is time to take these morsels of information as sustenance as you start down your road and fulfill your destiny in the annals of history.

Fare thee well, ungentle reader. May the moon shine upon you always.

# GLOSSARY

## ANKH

The Egyptian hieroglyphic that stands for "eternal life." Vampires over the centuries have adopted it as a symbol of their immortality, perhaps because many legends imply that ancient Egypt was the home of the first vampires.

## BAOBHAN SITH

Few mortal men stand a chance against this hypnotizingly beautiful, telepathic, and bloodthirsty seductress. Always clad in a green dress, she invites men to dance and then feeds on their blood.

## BLOODTHIRST

The intense, all-consuming desire for blood that can only be known by hungry vampires. Some vampires have learned to resist this thirst, but many cannot.

## CANINES

Four pointed teeth that help carnivores and omnivores tear and chew meat. In vampires, the two upper canines develop to be much more pronounced, allowing them to pierce their victims in two clean bite marks with minimal damage—and minimal evidence.

## CHIANG-SHIH

Blind undead that are products of violent deaths in China. The strongest of these hopping vampires can shapeshift and fly.

## CHUPACABRA

A legendary monster in Latin America, this bloodsucking beast has long been sneakily devouring local animals and striking fear into humans. Its name is Spanish for "goatsucker," as goats are this monster's prey of choice.

## COVEN

A group of vampires that cavort together. The members are usually related by bloodline, friendship, or common interest. Some covens stay together for thousands of years and have elaborate rules for membership.

## CRYPT

A stone burial vault traditionally built into the lower chambers of churches. Cold, dark, and quiet, these are perfect spots for the dead to rest in peace—and for the undead to chill.

## CRYPTOZOOLOGIST

A scientist who studies creatures of myth and lore that some humans consider to be fictitious, such as vampires, werewolves, and the Loch Ness Monster.

## DARK EMBRACE

The chillingly delicious lip-to-neck lock in which a vampire bestows immortality on a human by biting. A deep and lasting form of intimacy.

## DARK GIFT

The gift only a vampire can bestow upon a human, that of eternal life. The vampire who gives that gift is known as a sire.

## DAYWALKER

When a pregnant mother is bitten, her unborn child is turned and a daywalker is created. Daywalkers have the same powers as *dhampirs*, but are distinguished by their hatred of vampires.

## DEMON

A demon is the purest and least human form of a vampire. Incredibly strong and powerful, they are a deadly threat to less-pure vamps.

## DHAMPIR

These children of vampire fathers and mortal mothers are significant forces; they are gifted with vampiric powers, but do not share vampire weaknesses.

## DONOR

Any mortal who willingly allows a vampire to drink from his or her throat.

## DRAUG

These superstrong, undead Vikings crawl from their burial mounds with a violent hunger and can only be killed by decapitation. Animals feeding near the grave of a *draug* are often driven mad by the creature's influence.

## FAMILIAR

A human who desires to be turned into a vampire and who serves as apprentice in the hopes of being deemed worthy.

## GLAMOURS

The trickery of perception that vampires use to make themselves appear irresistible, easily luring their smitten prey.

## GHOUL

A demon in the form of a shapeshifting beast that typically dwells in burial grounds.

## KÊR

The vilest of sprites, these dark goddesses date back to ancient Greece, where they wrought havoc on village after village.

## LAMATSU

Birthed in ancient Mesopotamia, this daughter of sky god Anu is gifted with the power of flight. She fears the amulet of Pazuzu, a fellow god.

## MANANANGGAL

This type of vampire, native to the Philippine islands, appears as a beautiful woman. She can sever her body into two parts and savors the blood of pregnant females.

## MOROI

A vampire with a conscience. This creature possesses magical powers, but it may be mortal and is known to feed respectfully.

## PHANTASM

Something that can be seen but that has no actual physical existence, such as a ghost or an apparition.

## PSI-ENERGY

Psychic energy. Vampires who are very sensitive to the energies of surrounding creatures may use this energy to sustain themselves in lieu of blood. Such vampires are called psi-vampires.

## RABISU

The terrifying creatures that lurk at the gates of Hell, waiting to feast on new arrivals. The only thing that can harm this vampire is pure sea salt.

## RAKSHASA

A smelly, shapeshifting ghoul typically found near Hindu temples. It prefers feeding on pregnant women and babies.

## ROLE-PLAYING GAME (RPG)

An online game that allows you to assume the identity of a character in a fictive universe and interact with other characters in that universe. Perfect for the tech-savvy and imaginative aspiring vamp who would like to try out the vampire lifestyle but hasn't yet met a sire.

## Royal Vampire

This powerful breed of vampire, aided by the ability to read minds and dress well, has ruled over the entire undead community for centuries.

## Shapeshifting

Lucky vampires possess this ability to transform to resemble other creatures, a talent that is useful in escape and deception. Many other creatures—such as werewolves and witches—are also capable of shapeshifting.

## Sire

A vampire who turns a mortal by bestowing the eternal kiss. A responsible sire will take on the nurturing role of mentor in the new vamp's life, ensuring that he or she learns how to feed and hunt properly.

## Slayer

A slayer is a female with superhuman fighting powers who makes it her mission to rid the earth of vampires.

## Sprite

A varied and versatile type of creature, typically of elfin heritage, that lives in forests.

## Strigoi

In Romanian tradition, these immortals feed on mortals without hesitation or respect. The *strigoi* has red hair, blue eyes, and two hearts.

## Telepathy

The ability to read the minds of others and communicate psychically. Some vampires are gifted with this superpower.

## Tlahuelpuchi

Typically female and native to Mexico, these vampires with various powers live in secrecy so as not to pass on their curse to family members.

## Traditional Vampire

If they weren't wearing capes, it might be hard to distinguish these immortal hunters from regular humans—until their fangs sink into your flesh.

## Vampirologist

A scholar who is fascinated by vampires and studies their history, culture, and ways of life. Potentially a great resource for information!

## Vrykolakos

This Greek vampire arises from the grave if the deceased was buried improperly, had been excommunicated from the church, or was killed by a werewolf.

## Watchers' Council

A famous organization of humans that studies vampire behavior and trains slayers in the methods of vampire combat. Its members are highly educated in the ways of the Dark Realm.

## Werewolf

Typically a human who shapeshifts, often involuntarily, into an ultrapowerful, flesh-craving wolf. Vampires have a long-standing rivalry with these fellow creatures of the night.

## Witch

A creature that is capable of harming vampires with various supernatural powers such as the abilities to raise demons and cast curses.

## Yara-ma-yha-who

A tiny, tricky, red-skinned vampire that is native to Australia.

## Zombie

A once-human, undead creature that feeds on flesh. Though zombies lack the cleverness, finesse, and supernatural power of vampires, they are a pesky threat.

# For Further EDUCATION

## For Your Viewing Pleasure

It is almost impossible to keep up with the cavalcade of vampire-themed films and television shows. The list below will help you fill a bit more of your eternity. Check with your vampire elders before viewing any film: They may have wise words as to which films would best suit your stage of undead development.

### Films

*Dracula* (US, 1931)
*Vampyr* (France/Germany, 1932)
*Mr. Vampire* (Hong Kong, 1985)
*Near Dark* (US, 1987)
*Interview with the Vampire* (US, 1994)
*Vampire Hunter D* (Japan, 2000)
*Perfect Creature* (New Zealand, 2007)
*New Moon* (US, 2009)
*Thirst* (South Korea, 2009)
*Dead Snow* (Norway, 2009)

### Television Shows

*The Munsters* (US, 1964–1966)
*The Little Vampire* (Canada 1985, Germany 1993)
*Forever Knight* (Canada, Germany, US 1992–1996)
*Kindred: The Embraced* (US, 1996)
*Ultraviolet* (UK, 1998)
*Angel* (US, 1999–2004)
*Blade: The Series* (US, 2006)
*Blood Ties* (Canada, 2006)
*The Vampire Diaries* (US, 2009)

## More Literary Inspiration

The vampire canon is vast indeed. Consider the titles below for additional insights into the world vampiric. Again, it's best to speak to an elder, as some of these tomes might not fit with their plan for your education.

*Vampires and Vampirism*, Montague Summers (1929)

Saint-Germain Cycle, Chelsea Quinn Yarbro (1978–2008)

Vampire Diaries series, L. J. Smith (1991–2009)

*In the Forests of the Night,* Amelia Atwater-Rhodes (1999)

Cirque du Freak series, Darren Shan (2000–2008)

*The Historian*, Elizabeth Kostova (2005)

*Tantalize* by Cynthia Leitich Smith (2007)

*Dead Is the New Black*, Marlene Perez (2008)

*Thirsty* M. T. Anderson (2008)

# Index

First edition 2009

Library of Congress Cataloging-in-Publication Data
Gray, Amy Tipton, date.
  How to be a vampire : a fangs-on guide for the newly undead / Amy Gray.
1st ed.
    p. cm.
  ISBN 978-0-7636-4915-9
  1. Vampires—Conduct of life. 2. Teenage girls—Conduct of life. I. Title.
  BF1556.G73   2010
  818'.607—dc22   2009028517

14 13 12 11 10 09
TTP
10 9 8 7 6 5 4 3 2 1

Printed in Huizhou, Guangdong, China

A Weldon Owen Production
415 Jackson Street
San Francisco, California 94111

Candlewick Press
99 Dover Street
Somerville, Massachusetts 02144
visit us at www.candlewick.com

WELDON OWEN INC.

Group Publisher, Bonnier Publishing Group  John Owen
CEO, President  Terry Newell
Senior VP, International Sales  Stuart Laurence
VP, Sales and New Business Development  Amy Kaneko
VP, Publisher  Roger Shaw
Executive Editor  Mariah Bear
Editor  Lucie Parker
Project Editor  Heather Mackey
Associate Creative Director  Kelly Booth
Designer and Illustrator  Scott Erwert
Assistant Designer  Meghan Hildebrand
Production Director  Chris Hemesath
Production Manager  Michelle Duggan
Color Manager  Teri Bell

Special thanks to Kat Engh, Micheal Alexander Eros, Miranda Gregory, Emelie Griffin, Sheila Masson, and Frances Reade.

### Photography

All images courtesy of Shutterstock, with the following exceptions:
**Corbis:** 27 **Scott Erwert:** 11 (trees), 48 /4 **Getty Images:** 111
**iStock:** 13, 23, 28, 35, 50, 60, 63, 82, 91, 125 **Sheila Masson:** 84–85
**Picture Desk:** 41 (*Buffy the Vampire Slayer,* 1997 / 20th Century Fox Television / The Kobal Collection / James Sorenson), 46–47 (*Salem's Lot,* 2004 / Warner Bros TV / The Kobal Collection / Frank Ockenfels), 49 (*Dracula,* 1931 / Universal / The Kobal Collection), 58 (*Dracula,* 1979 / Universal / The Kobal Collection), 115 (*Nosferatu,* 1922 / Prana-Film / The Kobal Collection), 117 (*Vampires,* 1988 / Columbia / The Kobal Collection), 118–119 (*Interview with the Vampire,* 1994/ Geffen Pictures / The Kobal Collection / François Duhamel), 121 (*True Blood,* 2008 / HBO / The Kobal Collection)

All image treatment and photo collaging by Scott Erwert

All illustrations by Scott Erwert with the following exception:
122: Juan Calle (Liberum Donum)

Front cover illustration by Scott Erwert based on a photograph by Simon Podgorsek